SAVING ALICE

Naomi Graham is the best family lawyer in the country. But beneath her professional demeanour lies a broken heart. When the man who caused that heartache — billionaire ex-husband Toren Stirling — returns to her life after a ten-year absence, Naomi doesn't want to know. Their painful struggle to start a family tore their relationship apart, so when Toren reveals that he has a young daughter, Alice, it comes as a shocking blow. Not only that, but he's now fighting a custody battle — and needs Naomi's legal expertise to help him win.

GINA HOLLANDS

SAVING ALICE

Complete and Unabridged

LINFORD
Leicester

First published in Great Britain in 2019

First Linford Edition
published 2020

A catalogue record for this book is available
from the British Library.

ISBN 978–1–4448–4517–4

1

Hands full with her lunch, Naomi Graham pushed her pencil-skirted bottom expertly onto the door handle and reversed into her office.

'Good afternoon, Naomi.'

She knew that voice. Its deep tenor vibrated every bone in her body. She whirled around, and coffee flew out of the flimsy plastic lid. She swore, not because of the hot liquid rapidly seeping through her silk blouse, but because he was there, in her office, her haven, where no-one could hurt her again. Not even the man she had once vowed to love and cherish till death did them part. In the end it had been something much less bearable than death that had parted them.

'Here, let me help you. I didn't mean to give you a shock.'

That was putting it lightly. For

several seconds her body froze. Even years after their divorce she'd prayed he would turn up out of the blue one day. She'd scan crowds hoping to catch a glimpse of his face, knew exactly what she would say to him. Only recently had she given up thinking that could ever happen. Now, here he was, and despite all those speeches she'd rehearsed, she was incapable of uttering a word. Here he was, in the flesh. In the last place she'd ever expected to see him. Toren Stirling.

He jumped up from his chair, took the coffee and paper bag from her and swiftly stepped back again as if he thought she might take a swing at him. Part of her would have liked to, that was for certain, but she wasn't about to give him the satisfaction of stripping her of the dignity and respect she'd worked hard to build up since the last time she'd set eyes on him.

Instead, she shot him a look that said stay away, turned to her desk to pull a handful of tissues from the box and tried to focus on patting the stains on her shirt. It was a futile action but at least it bought her time while she fought to get her normally sharp mind back into gear.

'Toren,' she said, and tossed the sodden tissues in the bin with the same disregard he'd thrown away their marriage all those years ago. 'I didn't think I'd ever have the displeasure of seeing you again. What, in God's name, are you doing here?' She switched her brain to work mode; the coping mechanism she used to ensure the more emotional cases she worked on didn't get under her skin. If her words weren't strong enough to belie her true feelings, she'd end up a crumbling mess, and she wasn't going to let him do that to her. Not for a second time.

He placed the coffee cup and paper bag containing her sandwich on her desk and sat down. His long legs stretched out in front of him and she couldn't help noticing he'd maintained the lean, athletic frame that always made her catch her breath.

Clean-shaven, as always, and dressed in a sharp black suit that would put any dapper gent to shame, he hadn't changed much in 10 years. There was something about his face that was different, though — something Naomi couldn't quite put her finger on.

The obvious difference was his hair. It was still parted at the side and neatly swept back but instead of dark cocoa brown, it was now a sheet of steely grey. At 39 he seemed too young to be a silver fox, but she had to begrudgingly admit the look suited him, making him appear even more handsome and distinguished than he had before. If that were possible.

'Please, Naomi, sit down.'

Naomi? He'd never called her that. Even though they'd been divorced for nearly a decade, for some reason she still expected him to call her Mimi. The use of her proper name just served to remind her how long ago it had all been, how they, once inseparable, had become strangers.

A shot of the sadness she thought she'd long since buried leaked into her veins. No. She wasn't going to let him do that to her again. She was a different person now, not the sweet, love-drunk one she'd been as his wife. She'd changed — he'd made sure of that.

'How kind of you to invite me to take a seat in my own office.' She so desperately wanted to hold on to her dignity, to show him he hadn't totally broken her. But the pain was still too raw. It surprised her how much his presence blurred her judgement, tugged on her bandaged heart, threatening to chip at its patched-up surface.

'I haven't come here to fight, Naomi, I just want to talk.'

She swallowed and eased herself down into the leather chair behind her grand mahogany desk.

'Go ahead.' She rested her elbows on the plush leather desk topper and clasped her hands together to stop them shaking. 'I don't know what else there is to talk about, though. You seemed to say it all the last time we saw each other. The day you walked out, as I recall.'

He ignored the provocation in her tone and lowered his head into his hands. He pressed his fingers into his hair, and let out a shaky sigh. When he finally looked back up at her she had a chance to study his face close-up. His eyes, which used to be so twinkly, were bloodshot, like those of a man who hadn't slept for a month. She saw how those eyes, the very ones she'd looked into as they'd exchanged their vows, brimmed with tears, and her chest lurched unexpectedly.

In all the years she'd known him, even when they were going through all that rubbish, she'd never seen him cry. She had cried, more times than she cared to remember, and he'd stroked her hair telling her it was all going to be okay, that one day they'd have a child together. He'd pretended to be so strong but the emotional burden had driven him away in the end. He'd tried to be the big man but when it came to it he'd cracked under the pressure and left her when she was at her most vulnerable.

'Naomi, I need your help.' She stared at him, unable to compute his words.

A cloud of silence hovered over them. The only sound in the room was the relentless tick-tock of her office clock. He shifted in his seat. Asking her for help must be killing him. She should probably be enjoying seeing him squirm, but the longer she watched, the more the protective shell she'd built around herself weakened. The relentless tick of that clock chiselled away at it, threatening to expose the weakness at her centre.

She forced herself to speak, to bring this hideous exchange to a close, and get him out of her office before she did the unthinkable and broke down in front of him.

'You want me to help you?'

'I didn't expect this to be easy.'

A whiff of furniture polish caught in her nostrils and turned her stomach.

'Oh, I'm sorry this is difficult for you, Toren,' she said, aware of the facetious tone in her voice. 'Let me just get this straight. After six years of marriage, and as many failed attempts at IVF you suddenly decide you can't cope with the pressure any more, walk out of my life, file for divorce, don't contact me for 10 years, then come here wanting my help.' She shook her head and glared at him, eyes wide. 'Am I being unreasonable here?'

He blinked hard a few times. At least he was attempting not to do her the disfavour of crying in front of her. During their marriage, she'd sometimes willed him to cry, at least that would have proven he'd grieved the baby they couldn't have as much as she had.

He stood up and walked over to the window, his hands deep in his pockets. He looks like a little boy lost. She quickly shook away the sympathy encroaching on her conscience, and persuaded herself not to look away.

'No, it's not unreasonable.' He looked out the window at the Mayfair street below. He turned around to face her. 'Believe me, I didn't want to come here. After everything we've been through together, after the way it all ended. I realise I'm asking too much of you.'

'Then, why did you?' Her voice was calm and level, counteracting the shake in his. Thank goodness she'd practised that in the courtroom. Letting your emotions show when fighting a tough case wasn't the way to win. Nor was it the way to stand your ground in front of the man you'd once loved. The only man you'd ever loved.

'Because this isn't just about me. It's about someone more important, and to help her I needed to swallow my pride and find you. You're the best family lawyer in London, Naomi, everyone knows that. You're the only chance I have.'

Her head spun. He really had some

nerve. 'Ri-ght,' she said. 'I'm beginning to understand. You want me to help you get a divorce without denting your mass fortune?' After their break-up she'd made a point of never looking him up online. She always advised divorcing clients to do the same with their partners — wallowing in the past was counteractive to moving forward.

But the grapevine had no off button, and everyone in the City knew that Toren Stirling had sold his IT security company for millions, resulting in him being one of the wealthiest men in the capital. Not that she cared about that. Earning her own money as a top family lawyer was far more satisfying than relying on handouts from him. She'd even turned down his offer of receiving any monetary benefits in the divorce.

Once it was clear he wasn't coming back, she wanted to sever ties as soon as possible, not enter into negotiations about how much she wanted from him. She'd wanted nothing from him, and had taken nothing. Instead, she'd retrained in law at her own expense and lived in the most modest of lifestyles until she could afford better. Clearly the sacrifice had worked, as everyone — including her ex-husband — now knew about her reputation as a fierce family lawyer.

A lump the size of a golf ball formed in her throat, and she forced it back down. For a moment there she'd assumed he'd come back to find her because he realised ending their marriage had been a mistake. But no, it turned out he only wanted her for her legal skills, so he could free himself from whichever poor woman he had found after he dissolved their marriage. What a fool you are, Naomi. What a prize idiot. And only ever where Toren-bloody-Stirling is involved.

He returned to his chair, shunting it forward to get closer to her desk. He was only inches from her now but she resisted the urge to change position, even though a voice inside her screamed to get as far away from him as possible. She was in charge here and about time too. She'd spent her 20s trying to please him and look what that had got her — an empty womb and an even emptier heart.

'It's not another woman, Naomi. It's a girl. A little girl. My daughter.'

Her breath stuck in her windpipe. She took a moment to process the information, and when it finally began to make sense in her brain, she wanted to crease her face up and scream at him: I wanted to be the one to give you a child. Me. Your wife. Your childhood sweetheart. But in the end, it had been someone else. Another woman whose body did what a woman's body should. Someone else. Not her.

'You have a daughter?' her voice came out in a croak.

'Her name's Ali. She's just turned nine.' He smiled, an absent-minded smile. For the first time in their exchange, his eyes shone as if memories of happy moments ran behind them.

Her stomach turned inside out. Nine

years ago? So soon after our break-up. It was the gift she had spent years trying to give him and yet someone else had done it just months after they had separated — before the divorce had even gone through!

She coughed to dislodge the lump that had reformed in her throat.

'And what exactly is it you want from me?'

He looked at her again. His smile faded.

'Michelle, Ali's mother . . . '

'Your ex?'

'Hardly,' he laughed drily. 'It was a one-off, a stupid, drunken mistake at a party.'

She drew a sharp breath in. The Toren she knew didn't get drunk, or lose control, not ever. And especially not at parties. He'd hated parties!

'I don't regret it though,' he added quickly, looking straight back at her. 'I got Ali from it, so I could never be sorry it happened. Far from it. She's the best thing that ever happened to me. Well, one of them, anyway.' His eyes pierced into her, making her stomach sink to the soles of her stilettos. This wasn't fair. He was playing with her head. Was he trying to infer their marriage had been a good thing?

'Anyway, you were saying . . . Michelle?' She urged him on, not wanting to have to deal with the emotional whirlwind stirring up inside. She'd worked too hard at getting over him and making a success of herself to let it all come crashing down because he'd decided to saunter back into her life without a care for how it would make her feel.

'Yes, yes. Michelle. I've barely seen her since Ali was a baby. We were never together, not in the traditional sense after that one night. We only saw each other because of Ali.'

Naomi didn't want to hear about that night. She didn't want to imagine how Toren might have looked at another woman in the same way he used to look at her, didn't want to think his body had united with someone else's. Even after all these years, the thought of him making love to someone other than her was like taking a knife in the stomach.

'When Ali was three months old I brought her to live with me. Michelle was very young, just turned 20. She was only interested in going out partying, not having a needy little being getting in the way.'

Good God, what had the normally sensible and responsible Toren been doing having a drunken one night stand with a party girl 10 years his junior? Her mind flooded with questions, but she forced herself to keep quiet.

'I was awarded full custody,' he continued. 'I went around to Michelle's flat one day to pick up Ali only to find her soiled and screaming in her cot. It was heartbreaking.' He shuddered. 'Michelle was in bed, out cold from a hangover, in no fit state to look after herself, never mind a baby. I took Ali home with me, appealed for custody and I won. It's very rare for a father to be awarded full custody, you know.' He looked at her, slightly embarrassed. 'Of course you know.'

She gave a single nod without changing her expression.

'We've been happy together ever since. She's an incredible little girl.' He smiled, and puffed out his chest.

'So, you're a single dad?' Naomi had never imagined Toren as a lone father. Not that he wasn't capable. Even though she despised him for what he'd done to her, she couldn't pretend he wouldn't make a great dad. He was intelligent, emancipated, well read and hard-working, the perfect recipe for a good father — and husband. In theory, at least. She'd always assumed he'd go on to marry again and have kids, like normal people did. Him becoming a single dad had never entered her head.

'Yep. I had to make a few changes, of course, but it's all been worth it. I sold the business a few years ago. I'd built it up enough by then that it was worth enough to mean I don't have to work if

I don't want to. It means I can spend more time with Ali. I still consult for them occasionally when they need my advice, but generally only when there's a major client in town. Ali's my main priority now.'

During their marriage, he'd ploughed all his energy into work. She'd wanted him to cut down his hours, to be there more for her during the treatment but he said that working helped him cope. The knife in her stomach twisted. He'd given it all up now though, for his daughter, but hadn't done it for her. It just went to show how little she'd meant to him.

'You seem very proud of her. I'm happy for you. Truly I am.' She wasn't. How could she be when he had the only thing she'd wanted to give him but couldn't. 'So, what's the problem? Why are you here exactly if everything's so perfect?'

'Did it happen for you, Mimi? Did you have a baby?'

'Please don't call me that,' she

snapped. She hadn't liked the sound of her real name coming from his lips, but him reverting to his pet name for her when the conversation turned to babies was unbearable. It was a sign of his pity, and she wouldn't stand for that. Not here in her own office, her Toren-free zone.

'No, but it doesn't matter, really it doesn't. I wouldn't have time for a family now anyway, so it was probably all for the best. As a barrister, you see first-hand what can happen when domestic bliss falls apart. And it's not pretty, trust me.'

'I know,' he said, quietly, clasping his hands tightly together.

'But I thought it was just you and Ali? No wife to divorce, no teenagers wanting to disown you. I might not be a mother, but I can't imagine why having a happy nine-year-old would warrant the need for a barrister. And a very expensive one at that, I might add.'

'She wants her back,' he said quickly, as if the words poisoned his mouth.

'Michelle is fighting me for custody. Now, after all these years. She hasn't even made any attempt to see Ali in that time. They're practically strangers.'

'Didn't she ever want to see her daughter?' It was so unfair. She'd have given her eye teeth to have a child and yet here was a woman lucky enough to conceive after a one night stand, who thought of her baby as an inconvenience.

The familiar, disgusting bitter taste of injustice crept up her gullet, and she pushed it away again with all the will she could muster. There was no way she was going to let the venom of envy seep into her veins again. Her finger had moved away from the self-destruct button a long time ago and that's the way she intended it to stay.

'For the first few years I tried to arrange visits. But Michelle more often than not didn't bother turning up. As Ali got older she realised what was going on and would be inconsolable that her mother didn't care enough to see her. I decided in the end to let it go, for Ali's sake.'

'And Michelle never tried to get in touch?'

'Nope. Not once. Even though I always made sure she had our current address and phone number.'

'Didn't she fight you the first time in court? As you said, it's very unusual for fathers to win sole custody, even after a situation such as the one you found your baby in that day.'

'No. She didn't fight. She didn't want Ali. She had a new man on the scene who had a criminal record. Social services said their domestic circumstances weren't suitable for a child but Michelle couldn't have cared less. Without a baby in the way she could carry on as she had before, which was exactly what she wanted.'

'Then you have nothing to worry about.' Naomi leaned back in her chair and crossed her legs. 'It would take exceptional circumstances for a court to go back on their decision, especially if the mother has made no attempt to have contact with the child in all that time.'

'This is an exceptional circumstance.' His mouth formed into a thin, grim line. 'Michelle's saying she's not mine, that I'm not Ali's real dad.'

She sat upright, and stared at him. That was a game-changer. He was clearly besotted with the little girl he'd been bringing up for the past nine years, and now he faced a future without her.

'And are you? Ali's real dad, I mean?'

'I don't know.' He coughed and his cheeks flushed. 'It's quite plausible I'm not, given Michelle's, erm, lifestyle at the time. I've received a court order to take a paternity test. I have no choice but to take it, I'm just putting it off for as long as possible. All the time I don't know for sure whether she's mine, there's hope. If I take the test and it's negative, it could be game over.'

Despite every attempt to reel it back in, Naomi's heart reached out to him.

Now it all made sense why he had shown up in her office. If he'd tried to make an appointment, she wouldn't have seen him, he must have known that, so he'd come unannounced hoping she would agree to represent him.

'Toren, you had unprotected sex with a promiscuous party girl. What on earth were you thinking?'

'I wasn't thinking, that was the problem.' His blush deepened. 'It was just after you and I broke up. I went crazy for a while, couldn't think straight. Having Ali made me sort myself out again. I haven't touched another woman since. I have my daughter to think about now. She's the most important thing in my life.' His voice cracked, and with it so did a part of her.

She stared blankly at him but couldn't wrench her widened eyes away. It had never occurred to her that Toren might have been that affected by their break-up. He had been the one to instigate their separation, after all. And what was all that about being chaste for nine years? He'd always been a passionate man — abstinence wasn't in his nature.

'Right, well, you still have a very strong case. Even if you're proven not to be the biological father, you're the only dad your daughter has known and you won full custody rights for good reason. Michelle has every right to challenge that decision but her party lifestyle and ex-con partner will work against her.'

'She's sorted her life out,' he said, as if it was the worst news in the world. 'She married some hot-shot doctor last year and moved into his huge country pad in Surrey. I hear they've just had a baby son together and have obviously decided to complete their family by making Ali a part of it.'

'I see.' A fresh migraine began worming its way into her skull as she anticipated what was coming next.

'Where does that leave me, Naomi?'

He looked right at her with dead eyes and she realised what it was that had struck her as different about him. His once light olive skin had paled, as if drained of blood, leaving him with an almost vampirical complexion. Regardless of what they'd been through together, he didn't deserve to lose his little girl. She wanted to reach out and clasp his hands to offer him some comfort from the horrendous situation he was in. But protecting her own heart was the priority these days and she held back with all her might, clasping her hands together to resist the urge.

'With the biggest fight you've ever faced,' she admitted. Giving people false hope was never a good idea in the dirty business of family law. She'd learned that the hard way.

His eyes — sunken, dark holes — pleaded with her as he uttered the words she'd been dreading.

'I have no right to ask this of you, Naomi but, please, will you help me fight to keep my daughter?'

* * *

Her upper lip twitched, and her pupils flickered, and he was left in no doubt what his turning up unannounced had done to her.

'I wouldn't have come here, have put you in this position, if I weren't desperate.'

She folded her arms across her chest. 'So, I'm a last resort?'

'I could go to any lawyer in the country, but it's no secret you're the best. The only way I stand a chance of winning is if I hire you.'

She stood up, walked over to the window, and perched on the ledge.

He spun his chair around to face her.

'I sympathise with you, Toren. From what you've told me, this is a complex case. It's not a sure-thing that you'll secure victory. You do need a good lawyer, yes, and there are plenty around.'

'I want you.'

She glared at him, and he realised

that his choice of words weren't the most sensitive given their history. She stood up, walked over to her office door, and pulled down the handle.

'I'm flattered you have so much faith in me, but I'm afraid my case book is full.'

He stood up but remained at her desk, ignoring her hint for him to leave.

'I'll pay you double.'

She laughed, mirthlessly. 'You come here throwing your money around and think everyone's going to jump for you?' She shook her head. 'Unbelievable.'

'Naomi. Please believe me that I didn't want to come here today. I know what you went through . . . '

'What I went through?' She pursed her lips, and glared at him.

'What we went through,' he clarified. 'But that is not why I'm here. I'm here because I love my daughter. More than anything in the world. And I'll do anything — go to any lengths — to keep her safe with me. Unfortunately, yes, that means turning up here and no doubt digging up old memories you'd probably prefer were well buried.

'Please believe me when I say I wouldn't have done that if it weren't absolutely necessary. But it is necessary, because my daughter's future is at stake.'

'I think I've made my position perfectly clear.' She pulled open the door. 'Goodbye, Toren.'

He walked over to her and stopped just before he made his exit, then turned to face her. She tried to look away but he wouldn't let her, and angled his head so she had no choice but to meet his eyes. This quest was too important. He wasn't going to accept no for an answer.

'I know this hurts, Naomi, trust me, I feel it right here.' He struck a fist to his chest. 'Like I said, this means the world to me, and I want you. No. I need you. I won't give up until you agree. Not ever.' He reached into the inside breast pocket of his jacket, and pulled out a business card. He took her hand from by her side, and placed the card firmly into her palm, refusing to let go until she wrapped her fingers around it.

Her nostrils flared, and she stuck out her chin in defiance. He had thought the biggest fight would be keeping his daughter. Now he wasn't so sure. Without another word, he left her office, and walked down the corridor, hearing her door slam shut behind him.

2

She stared at Toren's handsome face, his smiling eyes and gorgeous grin, and took another swig of her drink. The over-sweet flavour stung her tongue. She gagged, then took another gulp. Her stomach burned in protest, but she continued to drink regardless. Anything to try and block out the emotions this afternoon's events had sent rampaging inside her.

She touched the photograph of her and Toren. She even remembered it being taken. They had not long since returned from honeymoon and their young bodies glowed golden after two weeks in the sun. His normally dark hair was punctuated with natural auburn streaks. Despite herself she smiled, recalling how their friends had teased him for having highlights.

They looked so sickeningly happy.

Her smile faded. It was like looking at another couple. A couple whose love for each other hadn't come crashing down because they — or rather she — hadn't been able to conceive.

She turned her attention to her younger self, staring back at her. If only she'd have known back then what was to come, she could have pulled the plaster off quicker, saving herself a lot of turmoil and years of broken dreams.

A sob caught in her throat. She squinted, willing on a tear, but her cheeks remained dry.

'Ha! My body's such a failure it can't even cry,' she declared to her empty kitchen. She tried again to squeeze out a tear but nothing happened. It was no use. She'd cried her last tear 10 years ago, when Toren had broken her heart the first time around.

Even when her parents died three years ago, and within months of each other, she'd barely managed a quiet weep. She'd been crushed at their deaths, there was no denying that, but crying felt so pointless, and she hadn't been able to do it even though she was desperate to, if only to help relieve some of the agony. Instead she'd busied herself with funeral plans and practicalities. At least that way she wasn't the dribbling mess she'd been when Toren had left. She couldn't go back to those dark days.

'You're quiet, Mrs Kettle. What do you make of it all?' she called over to the shiny black object on her kitchen top. 'Should I do it? Should I represent my ex-husband and his daughter, even though he left me because I couldn't give him a child? Ha, the irony of it all!' She paused her laughter, then frowned and cocked her head to the side. 'Oh, you think I should? So, you expect me to pretend all that heartbreak between us didn't happen? You're mad, you are, Mrs Kettle.' She snorted and took a swig from her glass. 'How would you feel if Mr Toaster over there let you go through six years — yes, that's six whole years, Mrs

Kettle, of excruciating, soul-destroying fertility treatment, only to pack up and leave when it didn't work!' She raised an eyebrow at the kettle. 'Would you reach boiling point?'

She slurred a laugh, and sighed heavily, turning back to the photo in her hand. 'I think I've finally reached my boiling point,' she said to no kitchen implement in particular. She traced the outline of Toren's face with the pad of her finger. 'And there's only one solution to this big, horrid mess.'

It was the last remaining photo she had of Toren — the only surviving relic of the life they'd shared. She'd burned the others when she finally forced herself to move out of their family home, six months after he'd gone, having given up hope he was going to stroll back in the door saying it had all been a terrible mistake, and that he'd never stopped loving her.

She hadn't been able to bring herself to throw this one away though. It was her favourite picture of them together.

They looked so happy, so natural, so full of hope for the future. So, she'd kept it. For some crazy reason her masochistic streak had taken hold tonight, and compelled her to remove it from the bottom of her bedside drawer, where she kept it well-hidden, take it to the kitchen table, and spend the last three hours poring over it.

No more. Enough was enough. She'd wasted six years of her life trying to make a family with this man, and the best part of the last 10 trying to get over him. Then, just when she thought she was getting somewhere, he had the audacity to show up again and catapult her life back into utter turmoil. The rip grated on her ears as she tore the photo in half. 'Well, isn't that bloody typical?' The rip had swerved to the side, leaving Toren's image perfectly intact and hers ripped through the chest. 'Still tearing me apart, and you're not even here!'

She slumped forward and pressed her forehead on to the cool table top.

'Decision made, Toren Stirling. I could no sooner represent you than fly to the moon.'

★ ★ ★

'Oh, dear lord. What on earth has happened to you? You look like you've been dug up.'

Naomi gripped the door handle, and squinted against the bright light streaming in from the hallway. The sleep-induced fog before her eyes began to clear, and she realised who had knocked on her door at this ungodly hour, waking her from her sherry-heavy sleep.

'Dee? What are you doing here at this time? It's the middle of the night.'

Her former colleague, who had over the years become one of her closest friends, widened her eyes.

'Middle of the . . . ? Are you kidding me? It's 9am. You know, the time we do our run in the park every Saturday? Just as we've done every week for the past five years?' Dee narrowed her almond-shaped green eyes and regarded Naomi.

'Darling, whatever is the matter?' she asked with her trademark rounded vowels. 'This isn't like you. You're normally up with the larks and Lycra'd up to the eyeballs by six.'

She swallowed, trying hard to quell the bile doing its best to force its way out of her gullet. 'I'm fine,' she whispered. 'Perfectly fine. I just didn't sleep very well. I'll get my running kit on and be right with you.' She went to move, but a wave of nausea swept through her, and she leaned on the wall for balance.

'Naomi, what's going on?' Dee pushed her way in through the door, took her by the arm, guided her to the kitchen, and steered her to the chair she'd just dragged herself up from.

'Drink this.' Dee set a glass of water down on the table in front of her. 'Well? Are you going to tell your best friend what's going on here?'

'It's nothing.' She sipped tentatively

on the ice-cold water, so as not to put too much stress on her already unhappy stomach.

'Nothing?' Dee shook her head so her long brown hair rested over her shoulders, and placed her hands on her slender hips. She looked around, surveying the evidence. A very large, empty bottle took centre stage on the table. It stood tall and proud like Caesar addressing his subjects — which in this case was a mess of empty crisp packets and sweet wrappers strewn haphazardly all around.

Dee picked up one of the empty wrappers between her finger and thumb, holding it at arm's length. 'Strawberry gummy bears,' she read from the packet, and screwed up her face. 'Naomi, you're the only person I know who eats quinoa for breakfast, and is happy about it. What's got into you?'

Naomi pressed the cold glass to her forehead, which had started to throb, and knew that resistance was futile. Dee would get it out of her somehow, and she hadn't the energy to fight it.

Dee had taken her under her wing when she first joined Blythe & Frazer Law. Back then, Dee had been the firm's most cut-throat criminal barrister. Clients paid through the nose to have her represent them, and her colleagues feared and respected her in equal measure. No-one quite understood how quiet, conservative Naomi, and Dee, a woman old enough to be her mother, and famous for her no-nonsense attitude, had become the best of friends, but they had.

Their friendship had strengthened even further in the last few years since Dee retired, and had more time free, a lot of which was spent advising Naomi on how to work her way to the top of the law game and still come out smiling.

She opened her mouth to tell all, but Dee spoke first. 'Hello, gorgeous. Who do we have here then?'

She looked up, and saw Dee

examining the section of the ripped photo which showed Toren beaming at the camera.

'Now, I could be mistaken,' Dee continued. 'But I'd say that Exhibit A suggests a member of the male species is responsible for you getting into this state. And a very handsome one at that.' She spotted the portion of the photo which showed a younger, smiling Naomi. 'Aha. A man from your past.' She bent down to take a closer look at the photo on the table.

'Wow, you sure have lost weight since then. Although, I must say, the extra pounds suited you. Perhaps you should dump the quinoa and eat sweets for breakfast more often.'

Something inside Naomi's stomach curdled, and she held her breath to stop herself from gagging.

Dee picked up the empty bottle from the centre of the table, and peered at the label. 'Cooking sherry!' She turned to her, open-mouthed. 'Dear God, Naomi. If you're going to get drunk on your own at least get some decent plonk in. You must have been desperate.'

'You could say that.' She couldn't think of the words to convey to her friend just how desperate for total obliteration she'd been last night. Once she'd polished off the remnants of the one bottle of wine she had in the fridge, she hadn't been in a state to walk to the shop, so had resorted to the only other alcohol available in the house.

Dee's expression softened. She flopped herself into the chair next to Naomi's, and lay a comforting hand around her shoulder. 'Who is this man, and what, pray tell, did he do to you that was so horrid you had to down a whole bottle of cheap booze to make it go away?'

She gulped, searching for a good place to start. Dee might be her closest friend, but she'd never even told her she'd been married. It wasn't that she didn't trust Dee with the information, it was just she'd always worried she might crumble if she allowed her heart to venture back to the time when it had been at its most fragile.

'Wait.' Dee patted her hand. 'I'll make us some tea first, then you can tell me everything. I think you've been keeping a lot of secrets, Naomi Graham, and it's time you shared those problems of yours.'

During mass tea consumption, she relayed the whole story to Dee, from her days being married to Toren, to his surprise visit yesterday. Dee listened, silently, taking it all in with a furrowed brow and only the occasional nod.

'So, what do you think I should do? Help a father and a child in need, or protect myself?'

'That's an easy one.' Dee slapped her palms flat on the table.'You cannot represent this Toren Stirling.' She spoke his name as if he were a notorious gangland criminal. 'You are too personally involved. It's against the professional code to take on a case you have a personal interest in. You know that.'

'Grey area though, isn't it?' Naomi said, dangling her empty mug by its handle around her middle finger. 'Although he's a figure from my past, I have no personal interest in his case. Far from it.'

'The partners might not see it that way. It's a challenge, that's for sure. And an interesting one at that. But is it worth risking your career for when you've worked as hard as you have? You're at the very top of your game, Naomi. Are you really prepared to squander it for a man who left you high and dry?'

She ignored the knot in her stomach Dee's warning formed. 'What about his daughter?Whatever he and I went through, there's still a little girl at the centre of all this. How can I live with myself if I refuse to help and she loses her father?'

Dee reached out to give her hand a squeeze. 'You are by far one of the best family lawyers this city has ever seen, but you have many competent colleagues, who can help Mr Stirling. If I were you, I'd give Piers Mandell a call. He'd do anything for you, and I'm sure this is a case he'd love to get his teeth into.'

Trust Dee to come up with a pragmatic, and helpful, solution. Why hadn't she thought of that? Piers was hugely successful. He came across as empathic to his clients, but was ruthless in the courtroom. Referring the case to Piers would give Toren a good chance of a positive outcome, and would mean her heart wouldn't be dragged through the mill in the process. Dee was right. It was a perfect solution. So, what was the reason for the brick of disappointment that sank inside her?

She moved her head nauseatingly from side to side until she spotted her mobile phone on the kitchen unit next to her. She reached over to grab it, then fished out from under the pile of debris on the table the business card Toren had forced her to take when he'd finally left her office yesterday.

While Dee topped up their tea, she texted Piers, leaving out the part about her having any connection to Toren. She simply told him she was referring the client because her caseload was already full, which was at least half true. Seconds later, her phone beeped. She picked it up and read Piers' reply:

Sure, Naomi. Sounds like an interesting case.

Shoot me the guy's number through and I'll give him a call.

By the way, have you thought about my offer of a second date? I really enjoyed our dinner together the other week. Let me know what time, and I'll pick you up x

She responded immediately with Toren's number, and made an excuse about already having plans for the evening.

'Is that Piers? What did he say?' asked Dee.

'He's interested in the case. He's also interested in taking me for dinner.'

'Well, go. It'll do you good to go out and have a good time — help take your mind off things.'

She started to shake her head, then gave up because it hurt too much. 'Can't face it today.'

'Do you like him?'

'I suppose so.' She shrugged. 'He's got the three 'S's'.'

Dee sipped her tea, and raised an eyebrow.

'You know,' Naomi explained. 'Solvent, sane and sober.'

Dee pressed a hand against her lips to stop herself laughing and spraying tea everywhere. 'I see you have very high standards,' she said, once she'd managed to swallow.

'Oh, I don't know, Dee. He's a nice enough guy. We understand the pressures of working in law, which inevitably means we end up talking shop all night.'

'Well, if you do like him, probably best you do take a rain-check on this evening. You don't look your best, darling. He might take one look at you and run away screaming.'

'Remind me why we're friends,' she said, and stuffed a biscuit in her mouth.

'Because I'm amazing. Now, get this problem of yours wrapped up, and focus on being you again.'

Naomi took the hint and picked up her mobile phone to text Toren. Contacting him was the last thing she wanted, but it would be unprofessional, not to mention unkind, not to let him know she was referring his case.

Toren, I'm afraid I can't help you, but my colleague Piers Mandell can. He's an excellent lawyer, and I can highly recommend him. I've given him your contact details and he'll be in touch soonest, Naomi.

She dropped her phone back on the table, and rubbed her still blurry eyes.

'Done.'

'Marvellous.' Dee clapped her hands together. 'Now, get in the shower, and put some clean clothes on. We're going out.'

'Oh please, no. I'm not up to jogging this morning.'

'Who said anything about exercise? You're taking me out for a slap-up brunch to thank me for my excellent advice. And quinoa is strictly off the menu. It's greasy spoon all the way for us this morning, darling. Desperate times call for desperate measures.'

Dee broke into a devilish grin, which Naomi couldn't help but return. Her friend's take-no-prisoners attitude had presented the perfect solution for getting Toren off her back, and not feeling like a major cow in the process. Now she could get on with forgetting him all over again.

3

Naomi snapped her work diary shut at the end of a busy Friday morning in the office, and mentally congratulated herself for successfully pushing all thoughts of Toren out of her mind whenever they'd threatened to creep up on her in the week since he'd made his unexpected appearance.

She'd deliberately made sure her assistant had filled her days with back-to-back appointments so she wouldn't have time to give him a second thought. For the main part, the strategy had worked, and now she was ready to grab a quick lunch before her final court session of the week.

'Want me to pick you up you some sushi, Lola?' she called across to her assistant before walking out the door.

'Oh, great thanks, Naomi. Just the usual please.'

'No probs. Back in five.'

She stepped outside into the drizzly London street, flipped up her umbrella, and negotiated her heels expertly down the puddle-dotted pavement. Although it was only the first day of August, summer already seemed to be a distant memory if today's weather was anything to go by.

'Naomi.'

She turned at the sound of her name, and her gut somersaulted when she saw who had called it. She wanted to carry on walking but her feet rooted to the spot on the end of frozen legs. All she could do was stand still and watch him walk towards her. His sharp, navy suit was drenched through, as was his Italian-cut white shirt, which clung to his body in a way she wished she didn't find so appealing.

'Toren. I take it you got my text? Has Piers been in touch?'

'Yes, to both your questions.' He stopped within feet of her. 'But I don't want him, Naomi. I want you.'

His shock of silver hair was so wet it stuck to his face, framing his rich, dark eyes. For a millisecond her better senses failed her, and she forgot he was referring to wanting her in a professional capacity. In spite of herself, hope soared inside her, then deflated just as quickly when she realised what he meant. He wants you to help him and his daughter, nothing more. Even if he did mean it any other way, there was no chance, no chance on earth, she'd put herself through that agony again. What was she thinking?

She straightened her back, opened her mouth, then closed it again. There was so much she had to say to him, such as how close she'd come to breaking down completely when he left; how she'd struggled during her training to make ends meet because she couldn't bring herself to claim a penny from him; how she'd lost every friend she ever had because they didn't know what to say to her when she'd hit rock bottom.

How could she get the full force of that across without risking a crack in her carefully pieced together dignity? If only Dee was here to tell her how to handle things. Or even Mrs Kettle. She would do, seeing as Naomi was doing such a shoddy job herself of dealing with her feelings towards Toren.

She plumped for the only way she knew — the professional approach. 'Piers is an excellent lawyer. I have no doubt he'll do you proud.'

The rain lashed down, but Toren seemed oblivious to the inclement weather. Water droplets balanced on top of his thick, dark lashes, and transported Naomi back to a time when they'd been together. On their way home from a night out they'd got caught in a heavy downpour. They held hands and ran through the streets to try to avoid complete saturation. The rain was too heavy, and in the end they gave up, and stopped in the street for a long, passionate, shelter-free kiss. The rain bucketed over them, but they didn't care. Even when her mascara ran and left her with smudged panda eyes, she hadn't worried. She was just so happy to be with the man she loved.

She looked at Toren's face now, sad and serious, and the optimism she'd built up over the week that she could forget him all over again blew raspberries at her and sloped off, leaving her exposed and vulnerable. She wanted to rip open her shirt, and peel away her skin to let him see her heart, bruised and battered, and force him to see the damage he was doing her.

'We need to talk, Naomi. Let me take you for lunch.'

Tell him where to go and leave him spitting out your dust, is what plain-speaking Dee would have said. And she would have been right. But, despite her need to protect her own sanity, her will to accept Toren's invitation was overwhelming. Why? So she could demand an explanation as to why, years ago, he'd woken up one day and announced their marriage over, leaving her emotionally desolate? He'd barely given a reason then, other than mumblings about there being nothing left between them. She knew of course the love had long since given way to desperation, to tests and being poked and prodded by fertility doctors, but she'd needed him, and he'd left.

With all the strength she could muster she forced the rejection from her lips. 'No, Toren. I know you're not a man who is often told no. And I know you like to have things your way. It was your decision to walk away last time. This time, it's mine. I'm going to walk away with my head held high. Whether you like it or not.'

She made to leave, but he reached out and grasped her arm. She swung back round to face him.

'Lunch, Naomi. Just lunch. There are things I should have said to you that I never did. I think you'd want to hear them.'

Curiosity gnawed at her resolve. She answered him quickly, before it ate her up completely. 'I can't. My afternoon is full of appointments. I don't like to let people down.' His slow nod told her that her pointed remark wasn't lost on him.

'Fine. Then tomorrow.'

She took in breath, ready to refuse, but he let go of her arm, and held his palm up to her..

'Please, Naomi. I don't blame you for not wanting to see me ever again. If for nothing else, think of it as laying some ghosts to rest. It might just do us both some good.'

She avoided his gaze, and chose a spot over his shoulder to focus on. He had a point. Or maybe she was just trying to convince herself accepting his invitation was a good idea, simply because she had an inexplicable desire to go.

'Look, just give it some thought,' he said, in lieu of her saying anything at all. 'I'll be in front of your apartment at midday sharp tomorrow.'

She looked down at her feet, and at

the point of her suede shoe, which was now submerged in a puddle of water.

'You don't even know where I live.' But as she raised her head, he was already walking away.

* * *

Toren turned up Classic FM and the cheery sounds of Vivaldi's Spring filled the Tesla. He drummed his fingers on the steering wheel and hoped the distraction of the music would save him from peering at his wrist and checking his watch for the fifth time since he'd parked in front of her apartment only minutes before.

He looked up at the sleek executive block, and wondered when she'd started liking modern architecture. This wasn't the Naomi he'd known. She'd loved characterful old cottages with period features. She'd hated the unified contemporary look that this building she now called home portrayed. Their dream had been to one day buy a house in the country, where their children would have plenty of space to run around. They'd fantasised about having an open fire, stable doors, a kitchen with a stone floor and an Aga . . .

Oh, for goodness sake. He had to stop his mind working overtime like this. He wasn't normally the nervous type, but when she was involved, well, that was a different prospect entirely. The last time he'd felt like this he was 15. It was the day he'd walked to school determined to ask out the pretty girl who had dominated his every waking hour since the moment she'd walked into his English class clutching her rucksack to her chest.

Not many people had shown an interest in the new girl. She was quiet, hard-working, unassuming, studious, but Toren saw the way her face lit up when she read out her report on *A Midsummer Night's Dream*. Her green eyes shone with a faraway look, as if she were in her own Fairyland, under the light of the moon. That was when he first fell in love with her.

Now at 39, his stomach turned over in the same way it had that day. He gave into temptation and turned his wrist around. Two minutes past noon and no sign of her. Maybe he should have taken her recommendation and called her colleague. At least he wouldn't be wringing his hands in anxiety waiting to see if some guy called Piers turned up for a meeting.

He glanced again at the swanky West End apartments. What if she's looking out the window to see if I'm here and can't spot me? Sighing out frustration at his own stupidity, he opened the car door and stepped out. Of course she wouldn't know what car he drove now. Several people came out of the door of her building during the time he stood there, watching and waiting. Every time the door clicked open his heart seemed to pause, only to resume beating with a heavy thud when the person who emerged wasn't her.

The broad face of his Breitling

informed him it was now almost five past noon. Naomi was never late. That was one thing he remembered about her. Ha! Who was he kidding? He remembered everything about her. Face it, she's not coming. He exhaled deeply, every molecule of air laced with disappointment.

He turned around to let himself back into the Tesla, and halted at the sound of heels on the pavement behind him. He resisted the urge to look, knowing he'd only be disappointed again to find out it wasn't her, and lowered himself onto the leather seat, closing the door behind him.

The sun glared in through the windscreen. He should have brought his sunglasses. A figure on the pavement only a short distance away caught his attention. He squinted against the brightness to work out if it was . . . could it really be . . .

It took him a few seconds to realise it was her. Although he'd seen her twice recently, her new, trimmer figure and short, elegant blonde hairstyle hadn't belonged to the woman he'd been married to. His young bride had long, light-brown hair and a curvier shape. Never overweight, but soft and lovely next to him in bed. The new version of Naomi screamed elegance and sophistication. She was polished and in fantastic shape. She was still stunning, just in a different way.

She wore a belted khaki jumpsuit, and looked cool and comfortable in gold kitten-heeled sandals. She met his eyes through the windscreen and started to make her way towards the car. He stepped out to greet her.

'You found me, I see.' She smoothed her sleek hair behind her ear. 'Not that I ever doubted you would. You always were unstoppable if you wanted something.'

Her clipped tone told him it wasn't a compliment. 'I thought you'd changed your mind,' he said, and walked with her to the passenger side.

'I never actually accepted your

invitation,' she answered, through glossy lips. 'You didn't give me a chance. You just assumed I wouldn't say no to you, like I expect no-one ever does.'

He opened the door for her and she climbed in, her long legs stretching out in front of her. He checked she was in safely before closing the door and going back around the other side to let himself in the driver's seat.

'You're right.' He cast her a sideways glance. 'The only person who says no to me is Ali.' He flashed a grin at her, which she didn't return. This could be a long day. 'Look, Naomi, I appreciate you giving me the time of day, but if you really can't stand being with me, then why are you here?'

She looked down at her hands on top of her lap. 'I'm not exactly sure myself. I can't represent you, I know that much. Let's just say I'm here for closure.' She turned her head to look out of the passenger window. He took that as his cue to start the ignition and drive. Only moments ago he'd felt like he had before their first date. Now, he realised, he could be preparing for their last.

4

'You're cold. Here, take my jacket.'

She was about to shake her head, but the luxurious silk lining of his blazer still held the heat from his body, and warmed her bare arms as soon as he draped it over her shoulders. It carried his scent. The same masculine cologne he'd always worn. The one she'd breathed in every day for a week after their first date when it still clung to the T-shirt she'd worn. She put off washing it for days because it smelt of him.

'If you'd have told me we were going on a lunch cruise down the Thames, I would have worn something a little more appropriate.'

'I wanted it to be a surprise. I know how much you love the view from the river.'

She sighed and folded her arms tightly against her stomach, protecting herself, not so much from the gentle breeze in the cool late summer air, but more from the effect of having him so close. 'Toren, what is this really about?'

Their lunch inside the boat had been civil, pleasant even. The conversation had flowed easily, although they'd stuck to safe topics, and hadn't yet ventured into the realms of what they were really there to discuss. She was aware the reason for their meeting would have to be addressed sooner or later, but she had liked the absence of conflict between them, and had almost allowed herself to enjoy his company.

Now, taking their coffee outside on the deck, as the vessel rolled past the famous London cityscape, it was time to address the elephant in the room, otherwise they'd be back on dry land before they had chance to broach the subject.

She didn't look at him sitting next to her on the bench, but was aware he was staring straight ahead, and sensed he was about to speak.

'Whether you choose to represent me or not, Naomi, there are things I think you should know.'

She shivered against the unseasonably biting breeze, and clenched her fingers around the edge of the wooden bench beneath her, bracing herself for what was to come. She shouldn't have come. It dawned on her that whatever he was about to say might leave her feeling worse. If they weren't aboard a riverboat, she could just walk away. She had been curious, but not anymore. Not now. She had a desperate need to be anywhere. Anywhere but here. Her heart pounded in her chest, and blood rushed through her ears. The start of a panic attack. She practised the coping strategies her counsellor had taught her. Breathe in, drop your shoulders, exhale slowly.

Her sweat cooled, and her head calmed. She trusted herself again to speak.

'Toren, if you're going to make

excuses for why you left me and started divorce proceedings, then I'm really not interested. What's done is done. I just want to focus on moving forward.'

He took a sharp intake of breath and, out of her peripheral vision, she saw him smooth back his hair. Buying himself time. Uncharacteristically, he was struggling to summon up the right words. He was always so calm. She almost felt sorry for him. Almost.

'You might think what I'm about to say is an excuse, but I want you to hear it anyway. If you decide never to talk to me again afterwards, then so be it, but I need to get it out of my system. I need you to know the truth.'

She gazed at the beautiful dome of St Paul's Cathedral, which stood majestically in the distance. So romantic, so ethereal. The perfect view for a tête à tête between lovers; the most bizarre setting for divorcees talking about their car crash of a relationship.

'You expect me to sit here and listen to all your woes just so you can get it out of your system? To make yourself feel better?'

'Naomi, please.' He held his hand out in front of him to quell her objections, even though she was sat beside him. After a few seconds of awkward silence, she cast him a sideways glance and gave a cursory nod to indicate for him to continue. Hearing him out might at least get him to leave her alone to get on with her life.

'I can't excuse my behaviour back then. What I did — leaving you when you needed me most — was unforgivable. I never apologised because I didn't think you'd give me the time of day to listen. I know it's come too late. I know it's only words. But for the record, I am truly sorry. I can honestly tell you, leaving you was the worst thing I've ever done.'

He placed his big, warm hand over hers, and gave it a firm squeeze. At his touch, an imaginary cape of warmth wrapped around her, like a favourite comfort blanket. She was giving in to him. No, no, no! She snatched her hand away and leaned her elbow on top of the plastic ledge behind her, twisting her body round to face him.

'Why did you do it then? Why did you leave me? Wasn't it enough for you that I allowed my body to be treated like a pincushion? Being poked and prodded and tested all the time. Trying to find out why I couldn't carry your . . . '

Tears stung her eyes, and she choked off her sentence. She turned away from him, focusing on the comforting familiarity of the landmarks until she gathered herself. Tears? She thought she'd cried her last, and here she was fighting them off.

The Shard spiked the clouds above the riverbank. Stoic and strong, it was everything she'd striven to be in the last 10 years. And now she was crumbling from the inside. Because he was back. Haunting her.

She coughed to shake off the remnants of the sob, and dared to look back at him. 'What is it you expected of me, Toren? I did everything I could to give us the family we craved. I would have adopted. We even spoke about that, but you left before . . . '

'I know. You did everything. That was precisely it.' He grasped her hand again. This time the comfort blanket came quicker, squeezing her tighter. She couldn't let go if she wanted to.

'What?' She tried too hard . . . is that what he meant? Tried too hard to give them the family they so desperately wanted? 'Would you have preferred me to sit back, let nature take its course and do nothing at all to help things along?'

The pause before he spoke was insufferable. She saw how he clenched his jaw, and his skin took on a grey pallor. Her chest tightened. What was going on inside that handsome head of his? What was it he couldn't say to her? Then his face relaxed into a weary, resigned smile.

'You're a tough cookie, Mimi. Sorry, Naomi.' His eyes flickered. 'You're much tougher than I'll ever be. That's what I admire most about you. You never sit back and do nothing. You grab life round the throat, and shake it until it gives you what you want.'

Her shoulders sagged. If there was something he wanted to say, he was holding back from it. She could push him, urge him to say the words, but the imaginary belt around her chest squeezed even tighter, warning her to stay on safer territory if she wanted to keep the approaching panic attack at bay. Another failure. She rounded her back and hung her head, squeezing her eyes shut tightly in a bid to keep them dry.

'Make life give me what I want, you reckon? I couldn't make it give me what I wanted then, though, could I? I couldn't control my own body's inability to conceive a baby.'

'No. No, you couldn't. And I couldn't sit back and watch the woman I loved put herself through any more torture.'

She opened her eyes and met his gaze. 'Then why didn't you tell me to stop?'

He smiled, a small, sad smile. 'If I'd have asked you to stop, would you have?'

She shrugged, unsure of herself. 'I never considered giving up. It wasn't an option.'

'Not to you. You're like a terrier. You're not a quitter.'

'But you wanted it too. Just as much as me. We talked about it, we agreed . . . '

'Naomi, I wanted a child with you more than I've wanted anything in my life. But watching you put yourself through that hell year after year killed me.'

She rubbed the heel of her hand into her forehead. 'Well, it wasn't much fun for me either. I don't remember you being the one doubled over in agony after they'd implanted eggs in your womb!'

He looked down at his hand on top

of hers, and stroked her skin gently with the pad of his thumb. The movement sent a shiver up her arm and all the way down her spine. Her head swam with a cocktail of pleasure and confusion.

Eventually he looked up at her and spoke. 'We were so young. I couldn't articulate what seeing you in pain was doing to me. Seeing you hurting yourself — your body as well as your heart — broke me. I blamed myself. I thought with me out of the equation you'd finally stop.'

Tower Bridge loomed over them, reminding Naomi she was just another tiny ant in this awesome city. 'Toren, are you trying to get me to believe that you left to do me a favour? Because if you are, you're completely, stark-raving mad.'

He exhaled, heavily. 'I know it sounds absurd. And it was a stupid, stupid thing to even consider doing. I can't tell you how many nights I've lain awake in bed, wishing I'd done things differently, wishing I'd talked to you, begged you to stop. I didn't want to be the one to make you give up on your dream, but nor did I want to be the one responsible for causing you pain because I couldn't give you a child.'

She snapped her head round to look at him.

'You couldn't give me a child?'

'If you remember, our infertility was unexplained. We didn't know whose body was letting the other down.'

She widened her eyes so much the cold air started to sting them. 'Were you afraid it might be you? You thought you were the reason we couldn't get pregnant?'

He wound his fingers between hers, picked up her hand and held it against his lips. He closed his eyes, but a single tear escaped before his eyelids managed to contain it. She watched it snake slowly over his cheek, and thought she actually heard the sound of her heart crack.

He opened his eyes again, and hastily brushed his thumb across his lashes.

'Ah, sorry,' he managed, and sniffed.

She resisted the urge to embrace him, even though she had to squeeze her knee until it hurt to stop herself.

'Yep. I guess I did,' he continued. 'I felt guilty watching you go through all that when I could have been the root of the problem. I thought if I left, you might one day get together with someone who could give you a child without putting you through all that punishment.'

'There's been no-one. I ... I couldn't.' Her words petered off, and the tears fell fat and fast. 'What a mess. What a bloody awful mess. Why didn't you just talk to me instead of suffering in silence and leaving?'

'I'm sorry. I can't tell you what leaving did to me. I was a wreck. I couldn't let you carry on hurting yourself like you were, so I did the only thing I could think of to set you free. I walked away. And I've been regretting it ever since. I never stopped loving you Mimi, never.' This time his eyes didn't flicker at the use of her pet name. He seemed not to realise he'd said it.

She looked over his shoulder as the London Eye came into view, and for a moment its painfully slow rotation hypnotised her. All this time he'd been in love with her, just as she'd been with him. The cruel reality of their situation sickened her. But it was too late. The damage had been done. It could never be undone.

'So, what now?' she said. Her nostrils caught a waft of boat fuel, causing a wave of dizziness to wash over her.

His hand let go of hers, and a rush of cold air filled her body, as if her comfort blanket had been cruelly ripped away. He propped his chin on his hands — a beleaguered man weighed down with a mountain of problems. She watched the gentle breeze toy with his silver hair.

'It leaves us 10 years on, both alone, both broken-hearted, saddened by the past and battling to survive the present. It leaves me with a daughter I adore and a war I can't win alone. And it leaves you facing a dilemma I was wrong to put you in.'

'It was cruel of you to ask me to help you after everything we've been through. But please don't think I can't understand how desperate you are to keep her. I couldn't imagine having a child then face losing them. Maybe that's worse than never holding your baby in your arms in the first place.'

He blinked and rubbed his jaw. The sight of him — strong, resilient Toren — losing his composure over his little girl, finally smashed to pieces the promise she'd made to herself not give in. She reached forward and placed a hand on his back.

'I'm sorry, Toren. I really am. I wish I could help you, but I can't. I hope you understand. Even though you regret how it ended between us, we can't rewind and do it all again differently. You can be as sorry as you like, but you hurt me, Toren. And I'm scarred.'

He nodded and wiped the back of his

arm across his face. She didn't owe him an explanation, but his silence compelled her to offer one.

'You think I'm strong? Maybe I am, but not strong enough to help you keep the child I could never give you. Perhaps that makes me spiteful, I don't know, but it still doesn't change anything. I've made my decision. You'll have to find yourself another barrister.'

He sat up, linked his hands together and cleared his throat. 'If that's your final decision, I respect it.'

'Thank you', she said. 'You know, you should give Piers a call. He's a damn good barrister.'

'Not as good as you.'

'Well, that goes without saying,' she said, forcing a meek smile.

Westminster Abbey with its two matching towers loomed ahead. Normal women had become princesses here, and yet for her it would always represent saying goodbye to the only man she ever loved. She didn't think her heart could sink any lower than it did when the loudspeaker announced their trip had come to an end.

He stepped off the boat first, and offered her his hand as she stepped down. Once she was on dry land he pulled her gently back, away from the path of disembarking passengers filing onto the crowded Southbank.

'I would ask if I could see you again, but from what you said on the trip, I gathered that request wouldn't be welcome.'

Oh, how easy it would be to say yes. She would see him again. She could look forward to their next meeting and even carry a faint glimmer of hope they could undo all the badness they'd let spoil their relationship first time round. But too much had happened for them to be able to go back. Don't forget the pain. Never forget the pain.

The lump in her throat strangled the words she was trying to form, and all she could do was shake her head. It was time to say their goodbyes. His eyes, still milky from the tears he had battled on the boat, shone down at her, dark and brown, and so devastatingly sad.

She closed her eyes to block it all out, and didn't think she'd ever be ready to open them again. His fingers, slightly rough, and warm, stroked a loose hair away from her face.

'It's okay, I get it,' he said, and ran the pad of his index finger so delicately down her cheek she wondered if she'd imagined it.

'Dad! Daddy! Dad!' The child's voice became louder until it was almost upon them. She snapped her eyes open. A young girl with a mass of unruly blonde curls was bounding towards them, her arms outstretched. Naomi looked behind them to see who she was running towards, only to realise they were the only people still on the dock.

She turned back and saw Toren had crouched down on to the ground, his arms open wide, and a grin stretched across his face.

'Dad!' called the girl again, just as Toren scooped her into his broad arms and nestled his face into her neck. Naomi gulped. That's all she needed — a real life reminder of what a cow she was refusing to help a young girl who faced losing her father.

'I'm so sorry, Tor. I did explain to her you'd be back this evening, but she insisted we came to meet you off your boat trip.'

Tor? Naomi turned her attention to the woman who had just joined them. She had a pretty, round face framed by a wavy, brunette bob. She was young, mid-20s, Naomi guessed, and wore a floral summer dress to her knees and a cropped cotton cardigan. Never touched a woman since Ali's mum, indeed.

Toren stood up, and rested his hands on the girl's shoulders. 'Naomi, meet my daughter, Ali.'

Ali grinned shyly at Naomi, and gave her a quick wave.

'And this wonderful woman is Pippa,' he said, gesturing at the attractive brunette.

She attempted a smile, but the effort

from it made the sides of her mouth ache. She hoped the smile looked more genuine that it felt — it wasn't Pippa's fault she was suddenly sick with jealousy.

'Pippa is our live-in nanny.'

Naomi's face relaxed, and the corners of her mouth turned upwards easier this time. Pippa smiled back, then jumped as a piercing ring came from her bright canvas handbag.

'Oh, excuse me,' she said, and stepped a few feet away as she fumbled in the depths of her bag for her mobile phone.

'Your friend's really pretty, Dad,' Ali whispered into Toren's ear loud enough that Naomi heard.

'I know, sweetheart,' Toren said, and smiled at Naomi, whose cheeks were growing hotter by the second.

'Is she the one in the photo?'

Naomi stared at Toren, fully expecting him to correct his daughter, and tell her she was mistaken.

'No, darling,' he said, but the pause

he left before speaking was too long for her to be convinced his denial was genuine.

'But, Dad, I'm sure that's her.'

Toren opened his mouth to respond to his daughter, but was interrupted by Pippa's return.

'I'm always doing that,' she said, and laughed, shaking her head at her own failing. 'By the time I find the flipping thing, it's stopped ringing.'

She seemed unaware she was the metaphorical bell that had saved Toren. Pippa pushed a wayward strand of hair behind her ear. The way it flicked up at the end suggested the action was a regular habit.

'She couldn't wait any longer to see her dad, and was driving me round the bend with her nattering to come and meet him.' The gentle, tinkly laugh which accompanied Pippa's words made Naomi instantly warm to her. She could imagine she was a natural with children, and that they adored her.

'Is Naomi coming for tea?' asked Ali.

'Oh no, no, I'm afraid I can't', she stuttered. Facing a judge and jury would be a walk in the park compared to having tea with her ex-husband, his daughter and her nanny.

'Orr, why not?'

'Naomi's a very busy lady,' answered Toren.

'Busy doing what?' pushed Ali, not wanting to give up easily on having a new dinner guest.

'Well,' said Toren. 'You know celebrities?'

Ali gave a serious nod, as if she knew many on a personal basis.

'Naomi is a bit like that in the area she works in. Everyone wants her to work with them, because she's so good at her job.'

'What does she do?'

'She helps families stay together,' he replied, planting a kiss on the top of his daughter's head.

Stay together? If only, she thought. Most of the time it was about helping them break up.

'Daddy,' said the little girl, giving her father a nervous sideways glance. 'Do we need Naomi to help us stay together?'

'Don't you worry about that, sweetheart.' Toren gave Ali's shoulders a squeeze. 'You're not going anywhere.'

Ali looked up at her. She was far from an expert in children, but even she could see how the little girl's eyes had dulled. Ali knew something was wrong. She'd heard it said that children pick up on things easily, and she'd bet her last penny that Ali was aware something was amiss.

Toren took Ali's hand in his much larger one.

'Bye then, Naomi. It was good seeing you again. Take care.'

Somewhere in her subconscious Naomi was aware of Pippa bidding her goodbye too, but she wasn't in any frame of mind for niceties. She stood, rooted to the spot, watching the three of them walk away. Pippa was ahead, and Ali walked behind, head down, hand-in-hand with her father.

Suddenly, Naomi was transported back to a time when she'd been around Ali's age, and had come for a walk along this very river with her dad. She'd adored her father, still did, even though he was no longer with her. She couldn't bear the thought of being ripped away from him, aged nine. How could she sit back and watch a little girl have her life turned upside down, unfairly, when she had the power to prevent it?

Before she had a chance to think things through, her legs kicked into action. She strode after them, while her heart banged against her ribcage, begging her to stop to protect its fragility.

If only she hadn't met Ali, she could have come to terms with her decision to walk away. But she had met her; had seen the fear in the little girl's eyes at the prospect of losing her father. She heard a voice calling out Toren's name. All too late she realised it was her own.

* * *

Ali's giggles washed over him as she played I-spy with Pippa in the back of the four-by-four. His daughter's laughter usually never failed to bring a smile to his face, but he was too distracted by the turmoil beating a painful rhythm against his temple for the beautiful sound to have its normal effect on him.

Naomi calling him back and agreeing — albeit, reluctantly — to represent him should have been a victory, but in the end it had caused a bad taste in his mouth. He'd intended on being completely honest with her — she deserved that much — but when he'd gone to tell her the real reason he had ended their marriage, the words got stuck in his throat.

It had all been true of course that watching the woman he'd die for put herself through the hell of continuous and unsuccessful fertility treatment had rotted his very soul. He hadn't been lying when he'd cited that as one of the reasons he'd chosen to walk away. Watching her suffer so much, so selflessly, to give him a child had almost been the undoing of him. He couldn't have let that carry on. Even worse was the prospect of adoption. In theory, he would have welcomed an adopted child just as readily as a child of his own. It was love that mattered — genes were irrelevant. But adoption meant risking allowing history to repeat itself. When he'd taken his vows and promised to protect Naomi, he'd meant it. In the end the only way he could protect her was to leave her.

He swung into their driveway, but still his mind refused to clear. The chatter from Pippa and Ali, the banging of their doors as they climbed out of the Range Rover, the light thuds of Ali's feet running to the door. It all sounded like it was far away, not happening here and now. For 10 years he'd carried his secret round, and still been able to function. Not cope exactly, but function enough he could make it through his day to day without giving in to the dark clouds that threatened to take him over whenever he thought about Naomi, and what he'd done.

Now he'd got what he wanted — persuaded her to act for him — and he had to come to terms with the consequences. They'd be working closely together for months on end until the case came to its conclusion. Just the thought of surviving that amount of time in close proximity to her while still harbouring his feelings for her, and the real reason he ended their marriage, was exhausting.

The dark cloud in his brain descended thick and fast now, and he gave in to it. In a matter of seconds, utter desolation had enveloped his whole body. He needed to tell her. She had to know. But what good would it do for her to find out now? It was too late. Far too late.

5

'Thanks so much for agreeing to come over, Naomi.' Toren reached across the kitchen island to hand her a cup of coffee. 'I know it's not ideal, meeting at home, but with Pippa visiting her mum for her birthday, and Ali being on summer holidays, I couldn't get child-care cover.'

'No problem,' she replied. 'I've been in court all week, so meeting out of hours suits me fine.'

Not wanting to put her in the awkward position of walking into his domestic life, he hadn't intended on hosting their first discussion as lawyer and client at his north London home. It had felt like rubbing her nose in it. But a week had passed since their trip down the Thames, and he didn't want to leave it any longer in case she changed her mind.

'Are you sure I can't tempt you to dinner? I'm cooking anyway, and there's enough for two.' He indicated toward the hob, where a pan of his signature homemade curry gently simmered.

'Really, I'm fine.' She began taking files out of a large handbag. 'May I?' She indicated to the kitchen table.

'Please. Use whatever space you need.'

'Where's Ali?' She smoothed the back of her skirt before she sat down.

'In bed. It's far too late for a little girl to be up.' He laughed, and instantly wished he hadn't when she shot him a disdainful glare. Of course, she'd have no idea what time an eight-year-old went to bed. He needed to be careful with his choice of words. The last thing he wanted to do was offend her, and give her reason to give up on him and Ali. He turned to the hob, and reduced the heat. He had no idea how long this was going to take.

'This should take no longer than an hour,' she said, as if reading his mind.

'Tonight is about fact-finding. I'm going to have to do some digging, I'm afraid. Some of the questions might seem intrusive, but I need to know the full story if we're going to win this case.'

He nodded. 'Ask whatever you need to. The important thing here is that Ali and I get to stay together.' A surge of acid shot up his gullet, but it wasn't hunger this time. What if he did lose Ali? The thought had never truly occurred before. He knew he was in for a battle, but had never before pictured himself actually losing her.

'I'll do everything in my power to make sure that doesn't happen.' Her tone was transactional, but sincere. He dropped his shoulders, and the panic eased. Whatever had gone on between him and Naomi in the past, she was a consummate professional, and he had every faith she wouldn't let their personal history get in the way of her job.

She fired the questions thick and fast.

Did Ali ever show interest in wanting to see her mother? How often had he tried to get the pair to meet? How would he describe his relationship with his daughter? Did he honestly not believe the girl would be better off with her mother?

'I think that will do for tonight,' she said finally, snapping the lid back on her Mont Blanc pen. 'You look tired.'

'Wow, a full two hours of questions.' He glanced at the digital time display on the cooker, and saw that a congealed skin had formed on top of his curry.

'Oh, sorry.' She turned her wrist to view her watch. 'The time ran away with me. I like to make sure I get my facts straight at the beginning. Last minute surprises aren't the way to win a case.'

'Listen, you must be starving,' he said, standing up as she did. 'It's 10pm. At least let me feed you before you go. I'm sure dinner is rescueable.'

'Honestly, Toren, I'm fine. I need to get go . . . '

'Da-ad!'

Toren lifted his head to look up the stairs, from where the small voice had come. Ali stood in spotty pyjamas, a few steps from the top, clutching a book to her chest.

'Ali, what are you doing up at this time?'

'Can't sleep,' she said, rubbing her eyes.'

'You look tired, pumpkin. Go back to bed, and I'll be up in a minute to tuck you in. I'm just seeing Naomi out.'

'Oh, hi, Naomi,' she said, doing an Oscar-worthy job of pretending she hadn't realised Naomi was there. She broke out into a bright smile, and descended the staircase.

'Erm, excuse me,' Toren objected. 'I said go to bed, not come down stairs.'

Ali skipped down the last few steps, and into the kitchen. Then she opened her eyes wide, and flashed him her best butter-wouldn't-melt look.

'It's no use, Daddy,' she said, shaking her head, her fine hair flying in front of her face. 'I just can't nod off. And you always say, it's better to read for a while if you can't sleep, rather than stare at the ceiling for hours.'

'Yes, but . . . '

'So, I've got my book ready.'

'Then, why aren't you reading it?'

She scrunched her mouth to the side and looked up.

'Because, I have an awake brain but tired eyes, and I need someone to read it to me.'

He glanced over at Naomi, and could see her suppressing a smile. Ali was playing him, and fooling no-one.

'Fine. Get back in bed, and I'll be up shortly. I'll read a few pages to you then.'

Ali turned her head away from him, and regarded Naomi.

'Would you read to me, please, Naomi?'

'Ali, no! Naomi needs to get home. She's been here a long time already, and I'm sure she wants to go to bed herself.'

'Please, Naomi,' Ali continued, as if she hadn't heard his protests.

'Ali! I've told you, no. Don't be so rude.'

'But it's a girl's book, Dad,' she pouted. 'You wouldn't understand it!'

He could do no more than stare at his daughter, open-mouthed. She never behaved like this, and yet here she was not only defying him, but acting the little madam.

Naomi bent down to Ali's height level, and took the book from her. 'Ah, Enid Blyton's *Malory Towers*. I used to love these books.'

'Did you?' asked Ali, her smile returning, even bigger than before.

'Yes. They were my all-time favourites.' She turned to him. 'It's fine, Toren, I'll read a few pages to her. I'd like to. It's decades since I've seen one of these books.'

'You really don't have to do that.'

But his words fell on deaf ears as Ali darted up the stairs, followed by Naomi. He was just about to shout after them, to warn his daughter not to have Naomi read too long, but the slam of her bedroom door came first. Little minx. He wasn't one to be outwitted, but he had to admit his daughter had just got the better of him.

* * *

Toren jogged up the stairs, a pile of Ali's clean, folded laundry in his arms. He reached the top of the landing, and slowed to a stop when he heard the murmur of voices coming from Ali's bedroom further along the corridor. Naomi's soft tones caressed his ear, followed by a giggle from Ali.

'This is my very best bit,' Ali said. 'Can you read just one more chapter Naomi, please?'

Toren tutted at his daughter's cheek, and made his way to her room to tell her enough was enough. He reached the doorway, and opened his mouth to speak, but the scene before him caused the air to lodge in his lungs. Ali was tucked in her bed, and Naomi on top of it, her knees bent, book propped up on her thighs. Engrossed in the story, neither of them noticed him. He should say something, or walk away, but instead he stood there, taking it all in.

To anyone else, they'd look like mother and daughter. Their honey blonde hair was an identical shade, and mingled together on the pillow, it was difficult to tell which of it belonged to whom.

His shoulders dropped. He gave his daughter everything within his power, but this is what she missed out on, and what he couldn't give her — a soft female body to snuggle up to, and a mum to do normal girl things with. Things, as Ali had so perceptively put it, he wouldn't understand.

He stepped back, bent silently to leave the pile of clothes behind the door, and retreated back towards the staircase. An intense ache filled his chest, and a waterfall of guilt rushed over him. This is what Naomi had craved, and he'd run away before they could achieve it. And now his own daughter was craving the same, and he couldn't deliver on that score either.

* * *

'Ladies, I brought you both a hot chocolate. I thought it would help you sleep, Ali, and I'm sure Naomi could do with a . . . '

Noticing the two figures on the bed weren't responding, he stopped short. Ali's arm was draped across Naomi's chest, and Naomi's hand was on top of hers. The well-thumbed hardback book lay, still open, on Naomi's thighs. Both woman and girl were breathing steadily, eyelids closed.

Toren smiled, sadly, guilt creeping up on him again. In front of him were the only two people he'd ever loved aside from his parents. Up until last week, they'd never even met each other, and now here they were, united in slumber, safe and warm and protected. With him. Together. Where they should be.

Be practical, man! He shook off the sentimentality, and considered his options. He could wake Naomi, but she was clearly exhausted, and he wouldn't want her driving through the city half asleep. Quietly, he placed the mugs on the bedside table, then turned back to look at the sleeping girls, wondering what on earth he should do for the best. He sighed, and rubbed the back of his neck. You sure get yourself into some situations, Stirling.

He walked to the side of the bed and, as gently as possible, hooked one arm under Naomi's bent knees, and the other around her shoulder blades, then scooped her up against him.

'I love you, Daddy,' Ali muttered from the bed, more asleep than awake, then turned over and curled her little body up into a ball.

'I love you too, pumpkin,' he whispered.

Naomi murmured, sleepily, in his arms, and nestled her head against his thumping heart.

'Come on, Mimi,' he said, so quietly it was almost a mime, and caught her scent as he held her close. It wasn't the same perfume she'd worn when they'd been married. It was beautiful, but much more rich and exotic than the scent she'd always favoured — the one he always bought her for Christmas.

Careful to keep his steps smooth and silent, he carried her out of Ali's bedroom, and into the neighbouring bedroom, usually occupied by Pippa. He lay her softly on top of the duvet, and stood to look at her. She was still wearing her full business skirt suit, together with blazer. It couldn't be the most comfortable to sleep in, he thought, but removing her clothes would not only disturb her, but also felt like too much of a liberty.

He walked around to the other side of the bed, picked up the edge of the duvet, and draped it over the top of her. She lifted her elbows from under the cover, stretched and yawned, then started quietly snoring. He smiled down at her. She looked so young and innocent when she slept — a million miles from the no-nonsense lawyer she was when she was awake.

'Goodnight, Mimi,' he mouthed, then left the room, pulling the door softly closed behind him.

6

Naomi lay completely still, and darted her eyes from side to side. This wasn't her pillow — it was much softer than her own. Her bedroom walls were magnolia not pale pink, and who were these people in the photo frame on the bedside table? She didn't recognise them. Wait. She turned on to her side, and leaned closer into the frame. She'd seen the pretty young woman in the centre of the photo somewhere before. Her sleep-fogged brain raced. It was Pippa, Ali's nanny.

She turned her head, taking in the unfamiliar surroundings. A short, black and white dress hung over the wardrobe door, a pastel watercolour of a seaside landscape hung next to the TV on the wall, and a jewellery figurine draped in bright-coloured bracelets and necklaces stood on the chest of drawers opposite the bed. This was Pippa's bedroom. How did she get here? And what time was it?

She looked around for her watch, and realised it was still on her wrist. She always took it off at night. Half past seven. An hour-and-a-half later than she usually woke up, even on weekends. Panic rose into her throat. She was going to be late for the office. She searched her hazy brain, and remembered it was Saturday. That was something, at least.

The last thing she could remember was reading to Ali. She must have fallen asleep, and Toren must have somehow moved her into Pippa's room. A sudden thought occurred to her, and she gulped. Tentatively, she peeled the duvet away from her body, and saw she was still fully dressed in her now very crumpled suit. She breathed a sigh of relief.

Ouch! Her left eye began to smart. Her contact lenses. She sat up, and quickly removed the offending lenses.

It'll all be fine, she thought, I just need to creep downstairs so as not to wake anyone, grab my bag, and let myself out. Yes, excellent plan.

She got out of bed, and was greeted by her reflection in a full-length mirror on the opposite wall. Her vision was blurred, but she wasn't so blind she couldn't see what a state she was in. Creased clothes, dishevelled hair and panda-eyed, she looked a complete mess.

'Oh, good grief!' she said to herself, and licked her finger before rubbing at the smudge of eyeliner that had somehow slipped from her eyelid to her cheekbone. She smoothed down her hair as best she could, then tiptoed out of the room, and down the stairs.

The blinds were all closed, and the house was silent. Safe in the knowledge she was the only one up, she hurried over to where she'd left her handbag on the floor by the table, and reached into the front pocket for her spectacles case.

She balanced the glasses on the bridge of her nose, and a gleaming black coffee machine perched on the kitchen worktop came into focus.

'Well, Mrs Coffee Maker. Although I could really benefit from making your acquaintance this morning, I really have to run.'

'Do you always talk to kitchen appliances, or just the ones you're friends with?'

She jolted back, and stumbled over the chair behind her. Toren. She had heard his voice, but he was nowhere to be seen. Then a silver head popped up from the other side of the kitchen island.

'Sorry,' he said, raising his hand, palm towards her. 'I didn't mean to make you jump. I was just looking in the cupboard to see if we had enough bread for breakfast.'

He wore a close-fitting grey T-shirt over tartan cotton pyjama bottoms, and his feet were bare. His normally sleek hair was ruffled, and a shadow of stubble covered his chin. Very sexy, she admitted to herself, and looked away as her cheeks started to burn.

'Can I get you a coffee? I'm sure Mrs Coffee Maker would be happy to oblige.' She could see out of the corner of her eye he was grinning, and her face burned more.

'No. No, thanks.' She lowered her head to her handbag, and rummaged for her keys. Where did I put the blasted things? She could never find them when she needed them.

Finally, she felt the cold metal beneath her fingers, and wrenched them out of her bag. 'Ah, here they are,' she said, more jubilantly than she needed to, and jangled them in front of her. 'I must get going.'

'Please, Naomi,' said Toren, a more serious expression on his face. 'Stay for breakfast. I really put on you last night, asking you to come here after hours. It's the least I can do. I'm making eggy bread — your favourite.'

She snapped her head around to him.

He'd remembered. Her heart lifted for a split second, before reality hit her like a punch in the chest. This wasn't her house, she wasn't part of this family, and he wasn't her man. Not anymore.

'I don't eat things like that now.'

His face fell, and she instantly regretted her harshness.

'Oh, I see.' He looked down at the loaf of bread in his hands. 'Well, thanks for coming over last night. Don't let me keep you any longer.'

He looked back up at her, and smiled, but his eyes didn't lift at the corners.

She spied her shoes in the hallway, and wanted to rush over, pull them on, and get away from this man, the beautiful home he'd made for him and his little girl, and the way he made her made her stupid, soppy spirits soar. But she couldn't cause a bad atmosphere, then walk away. Not when they had a case to work on together.

She stood on the spot, and shifted her weight to her other foot. 'Toren.'

She paused, unsure what to say next.

'It's fine, Naomi, I quite understand. You need to get going. Just please, get in touch when the case starts moving forward. You have my full cooperation. I'll do everything I can to make sure you have everything you need to win.'

'Well, thanks for, erm, your hospitality last night.' He nodded, and she walked towards the hallway.

'Daddy, my tummy hurts.'

Naomi raised her head towards the stairs, and was hit with a sense of déjà vu, but then it was only last night when Ali had emerged on the stairs, interrupting her previous departure attempt.

The little girl sat on the top step, her arms wrapped around her stomach.

'Really, pumpkin? Are you sure it wasn't because you ate too many sweets yesterday?'

Ali shook her head, vehemently. 'I feel really sick,' she whimpered, leaning on the stair post, and hugging it.

'Why don't you come and have some

breakfast, then see how you feel? It might be because you have an empty stomach.'

She shuffled on her bottom all the way down to the bottom step. 'No, Daddy. I couldn't possibly eat a thing!'

Naomi stifled a smile at Ali's melodramatic tone.

'If you're ill,' said Toren, 'it means you can't go and play with Mia Granger today, and her mum was planning on taking you both to Harry Potter World. You've been looking forward to it for weeks.'

'I know,' Ali's bottom lip started to quiver. 'But I don't think I'm well enough to go.'

'Okay.' Toren put the loaf of bread down on the island top, raked a hand through his ruffled hair, and exhaled. 'Right. I have a meeting today I can't get out of,' he said, verbalising his rapid thought process.

'No worries, though. I'll think of something. I could ask Mrs Collins next door if she'll sit for you. No, wait, she's not long out of hospital . . . '

'Are you meeting clients today?' asked Naomi. 'On a Saturday?'

'Yeah.' He drummed his fingers on the worktop, deep in thought. 'I cleared my week so I could spend more time with Ali while she's on school holidays. I don't do a lot of hands-on work these days, but an important client's over from Chicago, and I promised the new owners of the firm I'd see her before she flies back this evening.'

'Isn't Pippa back today?' Naomi offered, realising how difficult life must be for Toren as a single father.

He shook his head. 'Not till midday tomorrow.'

'Naomi could look after me,' chipped in Ali.

'No, Ali! Naomi's a busy lady, and she did enough for us yesterday.'

'Are you busy today, Naomi?' Ali asked, seeming to cheer up despite her stomach ache.

'Ali, this isn't like you. Stop being so rude!' blurted out Toren.

'Erm, not really,' Naomi admitted, thinking ahead to the day she had planned, which consisted of nothing more than going for a solitary run through Hyde Park since Dee had been whisked away for the weekend by her new gentleman friend. She'd probably follow that up with an afternoon and evening of case research at the office. She didn't have to work weekends, but rather keep busy by doing something useful than rattle around her four walls on her own.

'See, Dad, Naomi's free. She could babysit for me.'

'Ali! I've told you already to be quiet.' He turned to Naomi. 'I apologise on behalf of my daughter.' He gave her an embarrassed smile. 'Please, Naomi, don't let us keep you.'

Naomi took another step into the hallway, then paused. Toren's childcare issues weren't her problem, so why should she care? But then again, why not help if she could? She didn't exactly have an exciting day ahead. She spun around, and walked back into the kitchen.

'Listen, Toren, it's fine, honestly. I can look after Ali until you get back.'

He raised his eyebrows. 'Naomi, really, don't feel you have to. I'll think of something.'

She let her handbag drop from her shoulder, and tucked it in the corner of the kitchen. 'Leave this.' She indicated to the ingredients on the counter.

'I'll sort Ali out with breakfast. I'm sure once she smells eggy bread cooking, she'll change her mind about not being able to eat a thing!' She shot Ali a look, and narrowed her eyes, playfully.

'I might, if I try really, really hard,' Ali replied, in a small voice.

Toren looked from Naomi to Ali, and back again.

'Well, if you're sure,' he said, slowly. 'It would do me a huge favour.'

Naomi waved him out of the way, took his place at the counter, and rolled up her sleeves. 'It's decided,' she said, in her I'm-the-boss voice — the one she usually saved for court.

She wished she felt as sure as she sounded. She'd never been in charge of a child before, and hadn't the first idea what she was going to do to entertain her. 'How long will you be?' She attempted a care-free voice as she posed the question, and busied herself with cracking eggs into the bowl.

'I should be back around four. Is that all right? I could try and cut it short if you have somewhere you need to be.'

'No, no, four's fine.' She forced her facial muscles to pull her lips into a smile.

'Thanks so much, Naomi. You're a star.' He paused, as if considering what to say next, then pulled her in for an awkward, brief embrace, and planted a swift kiss on her cheek.

'Hurry up, then.' Flustered, she ushered him away, and pretended to focus hard on whisking the mixture.

*   *   *

'You look really nice.'

Naomi turned to the doorway of Pippa's bedroom, where Ali had appeared.

'Thanks,' she replied, turning back to the mirror, and smoothing down the spotty tunic top over plain black leggings. 'Are you sure Pippa won't mind me borrowing her clothes?'

Ali shook her head. 'Nah, she'd be really cool with it. Anyway, you can't wear a suit all day. How would we play?'

She put her hands on her hips, and turned again to face the little girl. 'Play? I thought you were poorly. When I was ill as a child it was duvet on the sofa and a bowl of chicken soup. There was no playing involved.'

Ali shrugged. 'I'm feeling better now.'

'Oh, that's good.' She glanced at her watch. 'Maybe I should call your dad, so he can let your friend, Mia, know. It's probably not too late to go to Harry Potter World. I'm sure you wouldn't want to miss out on that.'

'Well, it still hurts a bit,' Ali said,

rubbing her tummy. 'Maybe if we just stay in it'll get better quicker.'

She narrowed her eyes, and scrutinised Ali. 'Are you really not feeling well today, Ali, or are you avoiding your friend for some reason?'

'No way! Me and Mia are total bezzies.'

She smiled at Ali's incredulity at her suggestion. 'Okay, well, what do you want to do today?' Should she be telling Ali what they were going to do rather than giving her free reign to suggest anything? I guess when you're in charge of a child you need to think before you speak.

'Let's bake a cake!' Ali jumped onto Pippa's bed, and bounced excitedly on her knees.

'A cake?'

'Yes. I love baking, but Daddy's rubbish at it.'

'Don't you bake cakes with Pippa?'

'We haven't yet. Pippa's a good artist. We've done painting, pottery, scrapbooking, dressmaking . . . '

Jeez, was there no end to the woman's talents?

' . . . but, nope, never baking. I'm not sure Pippa can bake.'

'O-kay. I suppose we could.' She felt strangely satisfied that she was good at something Pippa might not be, then realised how uncharitable of her that was. 'You'll have to help show me where everything is in your kitchen, though. And we'll need to go shopping for provisions. Do you think you're well enough for a trip to the supermarket?'

'Sure.' Ali bound out of the room before Naomi could change her mind. She thundered down the stairs, and from the bangs and clatters, Naomi guessed she was starting to gather together every pan and utensil in the house.

What have I let myself in for? 'I'm not even sure I remember how to bake,' she said to herself. It had been a long time — years, in fact. She turned to the mirror and stared hard at herself. 'It's okay. You can do this. You're a perfectly capable human being. You face tough judges every day in court and win. You can bake a cake with a nine-year-old.' She laughed at herself. The last time she'd given herself a pep talk in the mirror was the first day of her job.

She glanced over at the bed, half expecting Toren to pop his head up from behind it, and laugh at her for talking to inanimate objects again.

'Na-o-mi!'

Ali was calling her from downstairs. Clearly, nine-year olds didn't possess the virtue of patience. She exhaled deeply, and headed out of Pippa's bedroom, in the direction of the kitchen.

* * *

'Your turn.'

Ali grinned, and wasted no time in scraping her teaspoon around the edge of the plastic bowl, gathering up as much cake mixture as she could. 'Mmm, divine,' she said, spreading half

115

of the spoon's contents on her chin in the process.

'Great word,' laughed Naomi, and took a much smaller portion on the edge of her own spoon. She savoured the delicious sweetness on her tongue. 'Gosh, I haven't eaten cake mixture for years.' She'd forgotten how incredible it tasted. And she'd forgotten how much she enjoyed baking. The relaxing methodicalness of measuring the ingredients, the satisfying monotony of the stirring — like therapy for her work-filled brain.

'Don't you make many cakes, Naomi? I thought you would do it all the time. You're such a good baker.'

She smiled at Ali, who smacked her lips together after shovelling another loaded spoonful of mixture into her mouth.

'I don't really have anyone to bake for. But I used to make them for your Dad all the time when we were . . . ' She stopped short, remembering that Ali didn't know they'd ever been an item, and she couldn't imagine Toren would appreciate her telling his daughter their sordid history.

'When you were married?' offered Ali.

She paused, her teaspoon halfway to the bowl, and stared at Ali.

'How do you know we were married?'

Ali raised her shoulders as if the bombshell she'd just dropped was no big deal, and took advantage of Naomi's hesitation by diving into the bowl with her spoon first. 'I heard Dad telling Pippa after he'd taken you out for the date on the riverboat.'

'That wasn't a date,' she said, attempting flippancy, even though her mind was whirring. What had Toren told Pippa exactly, and why was he confiding in his nanny? The jealousy she'd felt that day by the Thames returned with a vengeance, hitting her square in the stomach.

'What-ever,' Ali said, then pursed her lips, and tilted her head to the side as if she knew better.

'It wasn't a date, it was ... a meeting,' she said finally, wondering why she was so concerned about justifying herself to a nine-year-old.

'Do you think the cake's ready to get out of the oven yet?' asked Ali

Naomi got up from the kitchen table, and kneeled down by the oven to peer through the lit-up door. 'Another five minutes, and I think we'll be just about there.'

'Great!' Ali clapped her hands together, sending blobs of cake mixture splattering across the table. 'I can't wait to try it.'

'Only one tiny slice for you, young lady.' Naomi tapped Ali's arm gently with her spoon. 'You'll be sick the amount of mixture you've eaten. And you're meant to have a stomach ache. Your Dad's going to kill me!'

'He won't,' Ali said, a cheeky glint in her eye. 'He likes you too much.'

7

The moment he stepped inside the door, Toren was enveloped in the delicious warm scent of fresh baking. The sweet aroma filled his nostrils, and carried his mind back to the edge of another time. No matter how much he chased the thread of the memory, he couldn't quite place it.

He breathed in, and closed his eyes. Contentment washed over him, and for a moment he was happy to stand there, still in his raincoat and polished brogues, savouring the sensation.

'Naomi, Dad's home!'

Ali's call from the kitchen was like a dart hitting the bullseye of his memory bank.

Naomi. When they were married he'd often be greeted with the smell of baking if she got home first. She'd get in from work, kick off her heels, and leave them treacherously upturned by the door, spike-side up, as if she hadn't been able to wait one more second to get stuck into her favourite hobby of baking.

He'd dodge past them, into the kitchen, and wrap his arms around her waist. She'd bat him away, annoyed he was interrupting her at the critical moment. Always the critical moment. He smiled as the memory flooded back in its entirety. He wouldn't let go until she agreed to give him a kiss, and she'd laugh, amidst complaints the cake would get ruined, but would relax in his arms anyway, and he'd get his kiss. Several times they hadn't been able to stop at there, and the cakes had been ruined. But it was always worth it.

'Dad, come see what we made.'

He entered the kitchen, and took in the sight. Beautiful chaos. Pots and pans piled high in the sink, a magnificent, somewhat rustic-looking cake resting proudly on a plastic stand on the table, and his daughter and wife waiting expectantly for his reaction. Ex-wife, he reminded himself. Ex.

'We made you a birthday cake, Daddy!' Ali clasped her hands together in excitement.

'A birthday cake?' said Naomi. 'But your birthday's on the 29th of . . . ' She trailed off, her lips still parted. 'August,' she said, eventually. 'It's the 29th of August today, isn't it?'

'Yes!' replied Ali. 'Daddy's birthday! And Naomi said we could make you a cake, Dad.'

'What I actually said was . . . '

Ali butted in before Naomi could finish. 'And she said we should make a chocolate cake — your favourite!'

'I said we could make a chocolate cake. I didn't know it was your dad's favourite. Well, I mean I did know, but I didn't think . . . I hadn't realised that . . . '

'It looks incredible.' Toren shifted his gaze to the cake, in an attempt to save them both from further awkwardness.

Naomi obviously hadn't put two and two together and realised today was his birthday. At least he wasn't the only one Ali seemed to have got the better of.

'We can take it tonight, Dad, as pudding for our picnic. Naomi did most of it, so she should come and help us eat it.'

Naomi looked up at him, and their eyes met. They were locked in a bubble together, neither knowing what to say to get them out of this one. With her bright red spotted top, and flour-spattered arms, she was a world away from the hotshot lawyer whose office he'd entered last week. He had to stop himself wrapping his arms around her waist, tickling her until she gave in, and kissing her firmly on the mouth.

'I'm sorry, I can't. I have to get going.' With her words the bubble burst, leaving him crudely exposed to the reality of their situation.

'Of course.' He followed her into the hallway to see her out. 'I can't thank you enough for helping me out today.'

'It's really no problem.' She grabbed her coat from the hook by the door. 'Ali's a lovely little girl. I enjoyed spending the day with her.' She turned to face him, and for a moment too long, he stared into her eyes, and could see she meant it. Don't let her go. He rubbed his upper eye socket firmly with the heel of his hand, trying to force some sense into his head. 'Naomi . . . '

'I'll be in touch, Toren.' She turned away from him, and opened the front door. 'Once the paternity test results are in, I'll call you, and we'll go from there.'

'Already? I only took the test a few days ago.' The scent wafting from the kitchen suddenly seemed sickly sweet, and unpleasant.

'They don't take long to come back.' She pressed a button on her car key, and a silver Mercedes parked on the street outside his house responded with a click and a flash of its headlights.

'If the results are positive, Michelle

won't have a case at all, will she?' he called out to her as she made her way down his drive.

She spun round, and pressed her lips together, as if giving careful consideration to the words she should use.

'Most likely not, but I'd recommend you prepare for the worst. It will stand you in better stead for fighting your case than coming in the injured optimist.'

She waved, then turned away, and made for her car. When she was safely in the driver's seat he clicked the door shut, and rested his forehead on the cold panel. Prepare for the worst? How could he prepare for losing his daughter? He couldn't live without Ali. He couldn't breathe without her. He squeezed his eyes shut, and forced the sting of pain to retreat. He didn't want Ali seeing him like this. He gave himself a moment to recover, and returned to the kitchen.

★ ★ ★

'She's just so totally cool, Dad.' Ali had barely stopped for breath since starting to tell Toren all about her day with Naomi half an hour ago. 'She didn't even have to look in a recipe book — she knew it all off by heart, and she can crack two eggs at once.' She folded her arms across her chest and waggled her eyebrows, as if she'd just told him Naomi could speak eight languages and had won the Nobel Peace Prize.

'Wow, is that so?' he said from where he knelt on the floor, and tugged at the zip of the rucksack, which refused to cooperate due to the amount of picnic food he'd stuffed in there.

'Yeah,' sighed Ali. 'She's absolutely perfect, isn't she?' He looked up from the bulging bag to see his daughter standing over him, her eyebrows raised so high in a questioning look they'd disappeared under her mop of curly fringe.

A knock at the door diverted her attention. 'I'll get it!' She bolted out of the room.

'Check through the peephole it's someone you know before you open it.' He rose to his feet and went to make sure Ali wasn't about to open the door to a stranger, but he heard the whoosh of the handle, and realised she'd beat him to it.

'Da-ad,' Ali shouted from the hallway. 'Naomi's back!'

Naomi? She left half an hour ago. What was she doing here? Ali must have got it wrong. He turned the corner from the kitchen to the hallway. Sure enough, Ali was there.

'Is everything all right?' he asked. 'Did you leave something?'

'I'm really sorry to bother you,' she said, 'but I can't get my car to start. May I use your phone? The battery ran out on my mobile hours ago.'

'Come in, come in.' He ushered her inside. 'Have you been trying to start it all this time? You should have come in sooner. I could've looked at it for you.'

'I didn't want to inconvenience you. I know you were getting ready to go out, and I didn't want to hold you up. I still don't. If I could just use your phone quickly I'll call for roadside assistance, and wait in my car.'

'We've got a while before we need to get going,' he said, and slipped on his trainers laying by the door. 'Let me take a quick look first. If I can find the problem, I might be able to fix it for you now. You could be hours waiting for assistance to arrive.'

'No, honestly.' She held her palms up, fingers spread, her car key jangling off her middle finger. 'You've done enough for me letting me stay here last night. I can sort this out myself.'

Before she could object further, he unhooked the keyring from her finger, and snapped it into his closed hand. 'Go and grab yourself a cup of tea, while I take a look. It won't take a minute.'

She opened her mouth to resist just as Ali grabbed her hand, and tugged her gently away. 'Ooh, can we have hot chocolate instead?' she said, pulling

Naomi away from Toren, down the hallway.

'Erm, yes, sure. If that's okay with your dad.'

'Oh, he won't mind,' said Ali, disappearing with Naomi into the kitchen.

He smiled and shook his head at his little girl's attempts to play Cupid. As much as he admired her determination, he was afraid she was going to be disappointed that her matchmaking endeavours were destined to fail.

★　★　★

'It needs a new starter motor.' Toren wiped his oily hands on a tea towel. 'I could change it for you if we could get the right part, but I called the supplier and they're closed until tomorrow.'

'Oh, right. Well, thanks very much for doing that.' She put her mug down on the table, and stood up. 'If it's okay with you I'll leave my car here overnight, and get a cab to take me home. I'll call the garage tomorrow, and ask them to tow it to the workshop.'

'So, you can come with us tonight for Daddy's birthday! I'm so happy, I'm so happy!' Ali flung her arms around Naomi's waist and hugged her tightly.

'Oh, I don't know about that.' Naomi patted Ali's shoulder, wanting to let her down lightly.

'Look, why don't you come with us tonight? There's an outdoor movie on at the park. We were going to take a picnic. We've got enough for about 20 people.' He tapped the bulging ruck-sack with his foot.

'No. I really don't want to intrude on your family evening out, and I should be getting home. I've got so much to do.'

'It's Saturday night. You should come out and have fun,' demanded Ali. They both looked down at her. She'd stopped squeezing Naomi, and was stood with her hands on her hips in an old school ma'am pose.

'I'll run you straight home after the

movie if you like.' He resigned himself to his daughter getting her own way this evening. 'I'll swing by the suppliers and get the part and fit it tomorrow. It won't take long to replace. Rather that than waste your time getting a tow.'

'You don't have to do that, Toren.'

'I enjoy tinkering with engines. You know that.' He laughed, then regretted it. Of course she knew that. It was another reminder of their history.

'Yeah, he enjoys it,' said Ali, nodding vehemently.

'But look at the state of me,' she said, looking down at her clothes. 'Oh, and I've ruined Pippa's lovely top!'

'Ali, please can you take Naomi upstairs and get her some fresh clothes of Pippa's to wear this evening?'

'I don't think she'd be too happy about that,' Naomi said. 'I've already ruined one outfit. I'm sure she wouldn't want me risking another.'

'Don't worry about that,' he said. 'I'll give her a day off, and fund a shopping spree for her when she's back. She'll probably thank you for it.'

Naomi paused, as if thinking of more excuses she could use. After a few seconds she smiled, and held up her hands in defeat. 'All right, I'll come. If you're sure you don't mind.'

'We don't mind!' said Ali, before he had a chance to speak.

'Good,' he said, not sure whether it was or not. 'Better get going then.'

8

A thrill of excitement shot through her. A burst of coloured light appeared on the big screen, along with a crash of music. The film was starting. A giddy Ali had informed her, during the short walk to the park, the movie was to be *Labyrinth*. She hadn't seen that since she was a kid herself, and it had been one of her favourites. But to actually be excited about it? She felt a tad ridiculous about that, but smiled to herself anyway.

She snuggled down into one of the camping chairs they had lugged with them and stuffed her hands into the pockets of the gilet she had borrowed from Toren. It was miles too big for her, but she was grateful for it. Although the August evening was still pleasantly warm and light, she knew the cold would descend with a vengeance once the dark drew in.

'Popcorn for you, folks?' A portly, grey-haired man holding a tray of colourful bags asked.

'Ooh, Daddy, can I?'

'What? On top of the sandwiches, crisps and cake you've just eaten?'

'Pleeeeease,' said Ali, clasping her hands together. 'I ate all the crusts, even though I don't need to 'cos my hair's already curly.'

Toren laughed, and adjusted his position in the seat to extract his wallet from his back pocket. 'How can I say no to that?'

The popcorn-seller exchanged a candy-striped bag for the note Toren held out. 'And how about some for Mum?' He said, addressing Naomi.

'Oh, I'm not . . . ' she broke off, realising that telling him she wasn't Ali's mother would be information he didn't need to know. 'I'm not hungry, thank you.'

The seller nodded, ruffled Ali's hair, and moved on to sell his wares to the next family.

She cast a sideways look at Toren. He smiled at her, and offered her a chocolate from the box he had in his picnic stash. She shook her head, and smiled back, then turned to the screen. At least for the next couple of hours she could focus on the film, and avoid any further awkward moments. To the outside world, they must look like any other normal family, although the reality couldn't be further from the truth.

A giant owl flapped around on the screen, and the haunting melody of David Bowie's *Underground* rang out into the milky late summer evening sky. The song brought with it a flash of memory. It was the early hours of the morning, and the radio was playing. The smell of paint fumes lingered in the air. Toren was there with her. A sense of hope and excitement fizzed in their air as they decorated the flat they had just bought. The diamond engagement ring he'd recently given to her dazzled as she pushed the paint roller up and down the wall, and her chest filled with love and contentment.

Back in the present, Bowie's sultry voice penetrated her brain. She took her eyes off the screen and stole a glance at Toren. His profile was illuminated by the light from the screen. His steel-coloured hair appeared darker against it, and the worry lines etched on his face were invisible. He looked just as he had that night in their flat.

For one, glorious but fleeting moment, she allowed herself to believe they were still married, and Ali belonged to them both. They were here enjoying a movie under the summer stars, just like all the other families in the park. Then she blinked, and the fantasy shattered. She was here with her client, who also happened to be her ex-husband, and his daughter; the child he'd had to a woman he'd met at a party just weeks after their divorce. The hit of reality brought with it a mouthful of bitterness. She swallowed it, and averted her gaze from his silhouette.

* * *

'Who are you, and what have you done with Naomi?'

'What?'

Dee nodded at the glass of chocolate frappé on the table in front of Naomi.

Naomi smiled, picked it up and put the straw between her lips, then sighed in contentment as the smooth, creamy liquid slid down her throat. She shielded her eyes from the sun, and looked out onto Green Park.

She loved to sit here, outside the little coffee hut tucked away in a corner of the park. No-one noticed you, but you could see everyone else — all the families and tourists walking excitedly down the path, on their way to see Buckingham Palace. It was one of her favourite spots in the city. Even though it was one of the most popular parts of the capital, it felt a million miles away from bustle and smog. And today the flowers lining the park seemed more vibrant than ever.

'Weren't you the one, Naomi Graham, who told me you didn't eat chocolate? If I'm not mistaken, you said you might as well paint the chocolate on your body the way it made you instantly pile on weight.'

'I'm not eating it — I'm drinking it.' She put her lips round the straw again, took a victorious draw of her drink, then placed it back on the table. 'Besides, I'm treating myself.'

'So you should.' Dee delicately sipped her tea out of the paper cup, as if it were made of fine bone china. 'You're way too thin. Some womanly curves would do you good.'

She laughed. Dee was known for her straight-talking.

'Seriously, it's nice to see you looking chirpier this week. When you suggested meeting up for coffee, I was worried I was going to find you hugging a brown paper bag containing more cooking sherry.'

She picked up a napkin from the table, and pretended to swat at her friend. 'That was just a . . . a minor blip,' she said, silently thanking her lucky stars it had been Dee who had found her in that embarrassing state, and no-one else.

'It's because you took my advice.' Dee placed the plastic lid back over her cup. 'I take it Piers took on your ex's case with no hitches?'

Naomi looked down at her hands. She couldn't lie to Dee, but knew her no-nonsense friend would understand why she'd opted to act for Toren herself.

In the end she didn't have to lie. Dee was a professional at reading expressions. She'd built a career on it. 'Oh no. Tell me you didn't!'

Naomi pushed her sunglasses higher up the bridge of her nose, giving her time to ponder how best to explain why she'd done what she had.

'After everything Torrid did . . . ' Dee protested.

'Toren,' she corrected her friend.

Dee looked at her sharply. 'I was

describing him, not referring to him by name.'

'Right,' Naomi said, preparing herself for a well-meant dressing down.

'It's not too late to back out of it, you know. Just because you've verbally committed to represent him, doesn't mean you have to go through with it. You know as well as I do you'd be better to steer clear. If professional standards get wind of your relationship with him, they'd have a field day.'

Naomi shook her head. 'The contract is signed, sealed, and delivered. So, there's no backing out even if I wanted to.'

Dee gazed at her, silently for a few seconds, before finding her voice. 'Darling, you do get yourself into some pickles.'

Naomi pressed her lips together, not sure whether to laugh or cry.

'Well, if that's the case,' continued Dee, 'you've got some important rules to remember. Number one, only ever meet him at the office. Number two, conduct work in daytime hours only. And, number three, never meet his offspring.'

Naomi looked down, and scratched her hairline.

'Oh, Naomi!' Dee put her head in her hands.

'Three simple rules, and you've already broken one. Which one?' She snapped her head back up to look at her.

'Erm . . . '

'You've broken all three of them, haven't you?'

She took a deep breath in and out before answering. 'You could say that.'

Dee reached across the table, and clasped Naomi's hands in hers.

'Why do this to yourself, darling? After everything you've been through all those years ago. You're going to end up getting your heart broken all over again. Only this time, you'll have a muffin top to go with it.' Dee looked down at the empty frappe cup, making Naomi laugh.

'I thought you said I was too thin!'

'Yes, but that was before I knew you'd agreed to represent him. Now I know why you're letting yourself enjoy the finer things in life for once . . . because he's strolled back into your life, and you're getting all gooey-eyed over him.'

Naomi raised her eyebrows. For someone who had a reputation for being hard and unfeeling when it mattered, Dee was surprisingly perceptive.

'That's got nothing to do with it,' she said, grateful she had dark glasses on, so her eyes couldn't give her away.

'Just promise me you'll look after yourself. 'Dee squeezed her hand. 'If that man hurts you again, I'll throttle him with my Lycra leggings.' Dee smiled, but Naomi saw the flash of concern behind her friend's expertly made-up eyes.

'I promise.' She released one of her hands from under Dee's, picked up her cup and sucked on the straw, but there was nothing left.

9

Toren turned over his mobile phone and looked at the screen. Two hours since he had returned her car to her apartment, posted the keys in her mailbox and taken a cab home. And still no word from her. His own last message to her glared brightly at him:

Hi. Rang the bell but you weren't in. Car all fixed. Left keys in your mailbox. Thanks for joining us last night. Let me know when the test results are in and we can discuss strategy. T.

A few short sentences and yet they'd taken him almost 20 minutes to write. He didn't want her to think he was trying to get too familiar so had kept the language formal, but now he wasn't so sure. He frowned at the word strategy. Was it too business-like? Should he have signed off his full name rather than just use an initial? Should he have texted at all, or would a phone call have been better? He exhaled loudly and placed his phone back on the table face down.

'I'm turning in, Tor.'

He looked up to see Pippa peering around the kitchen door.

'Right.' He rubbed his eyes and realised how exhausted he was himself. 'I'll be heading off early tomorrow for the shareholders' annual meeting.'

'Sounds a riot,' she said. 'How do you cope with the excitement?'

'Well, I've hardly been counting the sleeps, but at least it's only once a year. After that I've got nothing planned until Ali goes back to school, so I can spend plenty of time with her.'

'Do you still want me to take her to town for new shoes?'

'Please,' he said and inwardly cursed himself for forgetting his daughter needed new shoes. Normally he was well organised with things like that, but what with the case, and Naomi . . .

Pippa nodded. 'I'll make it a fun day what with it being her last week of freedom before the start of term.'

'You're a star.' He swigged the dregs of his coffee and winced as the cold bitter liquid hit the back of his throat.

'I know,' she grinned.

'Night, Pippa.'

'Goodnight,' she called, already heading for the stairs.

He turned his attention back to his laptop screen. The words swam in front of his eyes. He needed to finish preparing his agenda for his meeting tomorrow, but his brain wasn't working properly. With a sigh he flipped down the laptop's lid. His phone buzzed and vibrated on the table to indicate an incoming text. He picked it up and turned it over. Anticipation caught in his chest, and he held the phone close to his body to put off identifying the sender. He shook his head at himself. What the hell was wrong with him? He glanced down at the phone screen. Naomi.

Thank you, Toren. Let me know how much I owe you for the car repair. Will be in touch once results in.

Nothing about their night out. No kiss, but then it was too much to expect that. Not even a sign-off. Still holding his phone, he brought his hand to his forehead and ran his thumb over the creases in his skin that had seemed to deepen in recent weeks. 'For goodness sake, Stirling, you need to stop overthinking this text speak. You're too old for this nonsense, get a grip.'

He stared down at the device in his hands and tapped the first thing that came into his head, determined not to analyse it for half an hour before pressing send.

No problem. Don't worry about it, it's on me. The parts weren't expensive, and it didn't take long. Just needed a new starter motor.

He stabbed send before he had time to think about it, then read the message back and instantly regretted it. He'd made himself sound like a flirtatious mechanic. He was still staring at the screen wondering how she'd take it, when the device buzzed in his hand.

I appreciate your help but don't expect you to foot the bill. I'll take it off your final invoice. Thanks again.

Well, that's put me in my place. I'm just another client. One she used to be married to, perhaps, but still just a client.

There had been a moment last night at the movie when he'd been compelled to reach out for her hand. The light from the big screen flickered across her cheek and highlighted her expression. She was completely transfixed by the film. Her lips were slightly apart, and her eyes were wide. She looked beautiful, innocent and vulnerable. For a millisecond the last 10 years floated away and she was still his. Reaching out to touch her felt so natural that his hand even left his own lap to stretch out to hers. He'd stopped himself just in time, and stretched down to the floor for the popcorn bag instead.

I'm just another client. He held down the power button until the screen turned black.

★　★　★

'Daddy's home, Pippa!'

Ali came thundering downstairs and threw her arms around Toren before he'd had time to take off his shoes.

'Hey, sweetheart. Good day?'

'Great day,' she answered, and squeezed her little arms around his waist.

'Hi Tor.' Pippa appeared from around the corner of the kitchen. Rather than her usual jeans and tunic, she wore a slim-fitting strappy black dress and high heels.

'Wow, you look lovely.'

'Thanks!' she said, and gave a twirl. She stumbled on her heels, and giggled. 'I'll never know how sophisticated women like Naomi wear stilettos every day. I can barely stand up in the things.'

'What's the occasion?'

'Michael's taking me out again.' She bit her bottom lip and smiled.

He frowned. 'The one with the motorbike?' Pippa might be in her early 20s, but that was still young enough to technically be his daughter, and he often thought of her as such.

She grinned. 'That's the one. The policeman. Anyway, don't you be worrying about me. If a young, fit police sergeant on a motorbike can't look after me, I'll have to look after myself, so it's a good job I'm pretty good at that!'

'I'll have a word with him when he gets here to tell him to drive slowly. Make sure you ring me when you get to the restaurant, so I know you're safe.'

She laughed, and put a hand on his arm. 'You're worse than my mum.'

'Sorry, I don't mean to be over-possessive, but you're part of our family and we care about you.'

'I know.' She embraced him in a hug. 'And it's so nice you do.'

He hadn't noticed Ali had extricated herself from around his waist to open the front door until he felt a draft of air hit his legs.

'Oh, sorry, I didn't mean to inter-rupt.'

Still holding Pippa in his arms, he looked over to their visitor.

'Naomi. I wasn't expecting to see you this evening. Come on in.' He released his arms from around Pippa, and gestured for Naomi to step inside.

'Hey, Naomi. Can I get you a drink?' Pippa grinned warmly at their guest.

'I don't want to get in your way if you two are on your way out.'

'Oh no, no,' he said, and held his

palm out to detach himself from the scantily clad young woman he'd just held. His embrace with Pippa had been entirely platonic, but it probably hadn't looked that way to Naomi. 'Pippa's the one with the hot date tonight. I have a night in planned with Ali and no doubt whatever the latest pre-teen girl sitcom is.'

'Oh?' Naomi raised her eyebrows. 'I thought you were expecting me. You said the only time this week you could meet was this evening.'

Toren stared at her, his mind racing. He would have remembered if they'd had that conversation.

'I called you this morning,' she offered. 'But it just kept going to voicemail, so I texted. Then you wrote back asking me to come tonight. I have to say it's not ideal to keep meeting out of hours but I'm really busy at the office this week so on this occasion it helped me out.'

'I forgot to take my phone with me today.' Toren turned around and saw his phone still laying on the shelf in the hallway where he'd accidentally left it that morning. He stood still for a while, trying to work out how Naomi could have received messages from him while his phone was here, and he'd been at work. Then it all made sense.

He turned to look at Ali, but she'd made herself scarce.

'Ali, come here now!'

A small, wide-eyed face popped around the door. 'Yes, Daddy?' she said, with butter-melting innocence.

'Did you send Naomi a text message today asking her to come here tonight?'

'Erm . . . ' she twisted her mouth to the side and looked up as if giving his question careful consideration.

'Let me think.' She tapped her finger on to her lips. 'Yes, I think I might have done, actually.'

'Why?' he said, exasperated that his normally well-behaved daughter would do such a thing.

Ali's bottom lip began to tremble. 'I saw Naomi's message asking you to go to a meeting, but I know how much you wanted to spend the rest of the week with me before I go back to school, so I asked her to come here tonight instead.'

He kneeled down, face level with hers.

'Of course I want to spend time with you, Ali, but you had no right pretending to be me. You know that's wrong, don't you, pumpkin?'

She hung her head and nodded, then looked up with shining eyes at Naomi.

'Sorry, Naomi. I hope you still like me.'

'No problem, Ali. And yes, I still like you.'

Ali smiled and wiped her nose with the back of her arm.

'Good. Then have a nice evening with Dad.'

Toren widened his eyes. 'And may I ask, what you have planned for this evening? I thought we were catching up on Teenage Witch School.'

'Ah.' Ali toyed with a strand of her hair. 'There was another text message that came in to your phone while you were out.'

'Ali?' he said, wondering what more damage his daughter could possibly have done in one day.

She pointed to the corner of the hallway by the front door. Toren, Pippa and Naomi all turned around at the same time, following the line of her finger. For the first time since he'd arrived home, he noticed a small suitcase against the wall.

'What?' he said, almost too frightened to ask. 'Booked yourself on a round-the-world cruise today, did you, as well as using my phone to arrange a meeting with Naomi?'

'Don't be silly, Dad.' She rolled her eyes. 'Mia's mum texted to ask if I could go over for a sleepover tonight. I knew by the time you got home it would be too late to reply, so I did you a favour and wrote back for you.'

'Oh, Ali.' Toren covered his face with his palms. Is this what it was going to be like from now on? Everyone said girls were difficult as they got older but until now Ali had never caused any trouble.

'Oh, there's Mrs Granger and Mia now here to pick you up.' Pippa said.

Ali looked hopefully at him. 'Can I go, Daddy? Please?'

Toren could feel Naomi and Pippa's eyes boring into his back, and for the first time since he'd been a parent, he felt at a total loss at what to do for the best. He was grateful when Pippa placed a reassuring hand on his shoulder and intervened.

'Let her go tonight, Toren. Mrs Granger is waiting. You can talk to her about it tomorrow.'

He paused for a moment, then wrapped his arms around his little girl. 'Okay. But you know you must never use my phone without my permission again, don't you?' She nodded her head against his chest, then pulled away and gave him a huge grin, showing a gaping hole where one of her front teeth was missing.

'Thanks Dad!' she said. 'Bye, Naomi!' she called, and picked up her case.

'Looks like Michael's here too,' Pippa said, and grabbed her jacket from the hook. 'I'll see Ali to Mrs Granger's car, then I'll be off. Have a good evening both of you.'

As if carried by a whirlwind, his daughter and nanny swept out in seconds, closing the door behind them, and leaving him and Naomi alone in the suddenly silent hallway.

*   *   *

'I think we've been had.' A faint smile played on Naomi's lips.

'I'm so sorry you were messed around. Ali's normally such a good girl. She's never done anything quite like this before. This is really embarrassing.' He ran a hand through his hair, contemplating the lengths his daughter had gone to in order to ensure he and Naomi spent the evening alone together. 'I'll quite understand if you want to leave under the circumstances.'

'Don't worry.' She slipped her cardigan off her shoulders to reveal lightly tanned arms. Her slim frame was hugged in all the right places by a smart white pencil dress. 'To be honest, meeting at this time suits me fine. I've got so much on at the moment that there aren't enough hours in the working day to fit it in. Anyway, I'm here now.'

Holding her large patent handbag in both hands, and with her cardigan draped around over her wrist, she cast a feminine yet business-like figure. She looked around, as if wondering where he might suggest would be the best place for their meeting.

'Come on through.' He stood back, and gestured for her to go into the kitchen. The glorious aroma of beef and garlic filled his lungs as he followed her. 'Will you join me for dinner this time? I was too busy to stop for lunch, and am absolutely starving.'

She opened her mouth to answer, and for a moment he thought she was going to decline, but then her stomach rumbled loudly.

'Oh,' she said, and put her hand quickly onto her middle.

'I'll take that as a yes,' he said. She smiled shyly in response, and a surge of pleasant warmth flooded through him. He didn't know whether it was the thought of eating the lasagne Pippa had prepared, or the prospect of sitting down to share a meal with Naomi.

She laughed lightly, her cheeks reddening underneath her summer glow. 'Thank you. It smells delicious. Did Pippa make this for you?'

He nodded. 'She most certainly did. And if I know Pip she'll have thought of this too.' He went over to the fridge and opened the door. 'And, voila!' He pulled out a bottle of chilled Sauvignon Blanc, and retrieved two wine glasses from the shelf.

'Thanks again for sorting out my car.'

She took the glass he handed her, and they took sips of the crisp white wine. 'Sorry I wasn't at home when you brought it back. I had to nip out.'

She smoothed her perfectly silky hair behind her ear. He remembered that mannerism of hers from when they were together. It was something she always did when she was on edge. She's lying. She had been there when he'd returned her car. She just didn't want him to know it. He took another sip, but this time the wine tasted like vinegar as it washed over his taste buds. His past behaviour had damaged her so much she couldn't even bring herself to answer the door to him. He swallowed, and the acid burnt his insides as it travelled to his empty stomach.

'Pleasure.' He forced out the word. The irony of its meaning compared with how he felt wasn't lost on him. 'I don't get the opportunity much these days to get my hands dirty. You know how much I enjoy working on cars.'

She looked straight at him, and once

again he regretted his words. Ten years apart was a long time, and yet he was talking as if she remembered everything about him. He fell silent, and was grateful when she spoke again.

'Did you ever get that classic car you were after?'

She remembered.

'No, unfortunately not.' He shook his head. 'They're not the most practical car to have when you've got a child.'

'No, of course.'

He hadn't meant to sound patronising, but he knew by the way Naomi looked down at her lap where she was nursing her wine glass, it might have seemed that way — as if he were making a point how little she knew about the practicalities of having children.

'Dinner must be ready. I can smell the cheese baking. It's a sure-fire way to know it's cooked!' He escaped the awkward situation he'd created by busying himself plating up their meals.

'Looks amazing,' she said, as he

placed a portion of bubbling lasagne in front of her. 'I think I need a Pippa in my life. What would you do without her?'

'What would I do without you?'

She looked up at him with raised eyebrows. Feeling he had to clarify his statement, he quickly added, 'Representing me, I mean. I know I've said this before, but I can't tell you how grateful I am. Ali is my world. I couldn't be without her. I know it wasn't an easy decision for you, agreeing to represent me, but I'm so glad you did. I mean . . . '

'Toren.' Her knife and fork clattered onto her plate. 'Please. I know how grateful you are, I don't need you to mention it every time I see you.'

'Right.' He picked up his napkin and wiped his mouth, as if the action would help stop the flow of his words, which always seemed to be wrong whenever she was around.

'It was a difficult decision to represent you, yes. Agreeing to help you keep a child when the reason we broke up was because I was incapable of having one was never going to be easy.'

'It wasn't about . . . '

'BUT,' her raised volume stopped him from finishing his sentence. 'It was a decision I made and that's that. I want to represent you, really I do, because it's the right thing. Now we need to focus on moving forward.'

'Sure,' he said, and proffered her the bowl of garlic bread slices. She shook her head. Welcome to no-carbs Naomi. She used to love bread. Could never get enough of it. He picked up his wine glass and stifled a sigh at the transformation in his wife. She was more ballsy these days, he'd give her that. Too ballsy? Maybe, maybe not. He liked her new-found fire. The way she'd shut him up just now was more than most people had ever managed. He didn't generally find people tried to shush him.

He swallowed a mouthful of meat. It reminded him of a flash in time, long ago. The memory came to him and he let out an involuntary laugh.

'What?' she said, a forkful of salad halfway to her lips.

'I'm just thinking back to the time you made us lasagne. Do you remember?'

Her cheeks tinged pink and she smiled. 'It was the first time I'd ever made it, and it turned out to be the last.'

'We'd not long lived in our flat, and we were still trying to figure out how to use the oven.'

'Yep. It was vile. But you ate it anyway, every morsel.'

'I daren't not eat it. It took you hours to cook.'

'Well, we didn't have a recipe!' she said, putting her hand in front of her mouth and laughing.

'Nope. No recipe but you thought you'd give it a go anyway. You always were willing to give things a go. I really admired that about you.'

Her laughter faded, and she looked down at her plate.

There you go again, you idiot, saying the wrong thing. What was it about being in her presence that turned him into a blabbering oaf? He seemed to lose the ability to think straight whenever she was around.

'Top up?' He held the wine bottle over her glass.

'No-no. Thank you but I'm driving.'

He topped up his own glass as silence fell once more.

'We had some good times, didn't we?'

She shot him a glance from under her lashes. Not wanting to get back into dangerous territory he picked up his glass. 'All I mean is, it's good to be on the same team again, albeit in a different way this time. We're both fighting for the same cause, and that's what counts. Cheers.'

She held her glass up to his. 'Cheers.'

'How about some pudding?'

'She makes you pudding too?'

'Yes, but it's not quite as good as your cake. Don't tell Pippa that though

— I'll be nanny-less!' He winked, and she smiled, showing her perfectly straight teeth. 'Thanks, but I don't think I could eat another thing.'

'Then how about coffee?' He scraped back his chair, stood up and flicked on the coffee machine.

'Toren, I know you might not want to talk about it, but we really do need to discuss about the results of the paternity test.'

A bead of sweat prickled his brow. He squeezed the coffee pod in his fist, not realising how hard until it burst in his hand, and shot its powdery contents over his skin. Slowly, he walked back over to his chair and sat down.

'You're right,' he said. 'I know I need to face reality. I'm just not sure I want to.'

* * *

Naomi had delivered many pieces of news to many families, and although it was never easy, this was the most difficult she'd ever experienced. She opened her mouth to speak but the words caught in her throat. His eyes, wild and swimming with unshed tears, searched hers. She could see he already knew the answer, but he still needed her to confirm it. For the first time in her professional career, she had to look away to deliver the news.

'The paternity test results show . . . ' she almost choked on her words, and had to cough before she continued. ' . . . that Ali isn't your daughter.'

His silence disturbed her more than any amount of shouting or cursing could have done, and instinctively she turned to him. He sat upright, stock still, facing her with his palms flat on the table. He hadn't moved an inch since she'd broken the news. His eyes were closed. Before she could think about it, her hand went out to his knee under the table. The heat from his body sent a zing all the way up her arm, even through the fabric of his suit trousers. Uncomfortable with how the physical contact with him made her feel, she snatched her hand away quickly.

He still didn't open his eyes, but brought his hand up to his forehead, and rubbed it hard, as if trying to make sense of the information he'd just been fed.

'No . . . ' he said at last, pronouncing every phonic slowly and carefully. 'No, no, no . . . '

Her heart hammered in her chest. Never in all their history had she seen him unable to control his reactions. And yet, here he was in front of her, looking like he'd been dealt a death sentence.

'Toren,' she said, trying to snap him out of this uncharacteristic reaction.

'Oh, Christ.' He brought his other hand up to join the first and dug all his fingertips into his hairline.

Automatically, she stood up, square in front of him and placed her hands on his shoulders. Without warning he wrapped his arms around her waist and pushed his head into her stomach. His reaction took her by surprise, and instinctively she lifted her hands away. Realising there was nowhere else to put them, she allowed them to drape loosely around his neck.

He didn't speak. Unsure what she could say to make the situation any better, neither did she. In lieu of knowing what else to do, she stood there, letting him hug her, and felt the rise and fall of his body as he took long, controlled breaths. In a bid to soothe him, she rubbed her arm up and down his upper back. This is the least professional thing you've ever done. Despite knowing better, she didn't stop. She couldn't bear to see him like that again; broken and shattered. That look on his face when she delivered the last news in the world he wanted to hear, would haunt her forever.

Eventually, he tipped his head back, his chin resting on her stomach, and looked up at her. She lowered her head, and their eyes met.

'I knew,' he said. 'I knew. But it still hurts.'

'It's okay.' She placed her hands on his head, needing him to listen to her next words. 'It doesn't mean you're not her dad. You'll always be her dad. It's just biology. It doesn't change the way you feel about her, or the way she feels about you. It's just genes. It doesn't matter.'

He pressed his lips together, and gave a humourless laugh through his nose. 'It does matter though, doesn't it? It matters more than anything. Because it weakens my case.'

Still holding his head, she bent down so her face was level with his. 'We can still win this, Toren. You have to believe we can still win.'

'We?' It was only one word, but it was a word loaded with hope.

She took a deep breath in and licked her lips. She couldn't have handled this worse if she'd tried. What the hell are you saying? You know better than this. She'd worked on many difficult cases before, but always managed to remain emotionally detached. This was the last case she ought to be getting caught up in. Not only had she managed to throw professionalism out of the window, she'd also somehow managed to end up in an embrace with her client. But she couldn't pull back now, not when there was a hint of optimism in his voice.

'Yes. We. I'm vested in this case professionally. Losing is not my style.'

Something in his eyes flickered as she said professionally. As if he'd been hoping her involvement might be more emotional.

He took his arms away from her waist, and hung his head. Her arms, still around his neck, felt suddenly awkward. She released her hold on him and gave his shoulders a quick pat. 'Let me get the coffees. I think you need a little something in yours to help with the shock.'

His top-of-the-range coffee machine looked complicated, but she figured it out, and after a few minutes, had produced two strong, black Americanos. She found a bottle of whisky in the corner on the counter, and topped his mug up with a generous dram.

'I need some fresh air.' He rose from his chair to his full six-foot three height. 'Do you mind if we take these out on to the patio?'

'Of course.' She let him lead the way out of the French doors. Now it was early September, there were signs of autumn setting in, and a distinct chill threatened the calm evening air. She placed the mugs on the outside table top, and took a seat as he lit the chimenea.

'It'll take a while to warm up. Take a blanket if you're cold.' He handed her the large fleece, which had been folded on one of the chairs, and sat down in the vacant space it left. She took it, and took the seat next to his.

'Thanks.' She wrapped the blanket around her body. It was so long it went from her shoulders to her ankles. She shivered as she adjusted to the temperature and leaned back against the wooden chair. The stress and adrenaline that had raced through her earlier when she'd delivered the news to Toren, began to subside, and exhaustion flooded her bones.

She watched him bring the coffee mug to his lips and take a sip before leaning forward to place it back on the table. The flame from the chiminea glowed in the dusk-filled air, and bathed his face in a warm light. His greying stubble looked blonde against the glow of the orange, and something pinged in her chest, like the twang of a guitar string. Cute or gorgeous he definitely wasn't, but he was suave in the same way that 50s movie stars were. He was smart, sophisticated and with a masculine elegance that so few men possessed.

As if he could feel her eyes on him, he turned towards her. She wanted to look away, so he wouldn't know she'd been watching him, but something stopped her, and she kept her gaze fixed to him until his eyes locked with hers.

'Naomi.' She wasn't certain if he'd said her name, or whether she'd imagined it as he laid his hand, big and heavy, on her lap over the blanket. Her thigh beneath zinged with the heat from his skin, which radiated upwards until her entire body was bathed in his warmth. He was leaning closer and closer to her. There was only one way this was going, and she couldn't let it. She should stop him. Lean away, put out her palms and push on his chest, open her mouth and tell him no.

He was so close now she could pick up the scent of his breath — rich coffee and whisky — against the soft black liquorice of his cologne. Any fight she might have had in her to object faded away. She closed her eyes, and waited for his lips to land on her own. They arrived, soft and warm, and with them gloriously bright lights went off in her head.

He barely moved at first, just gently

held his mouth against hers. Then slowly, cautiously, as if venturing into new territory, he began to explore her lips. His arms found their way around her back, and he pulled her as close to him as their seated positions allowed. She rested her hands on his upper arms, and felt his muscles tense beneath his cotton shirt. Their mouths didn't part, and she could barely breathe, but realising she'd rather collapse in his arms than break away, she took in as much air as she could through her nose, and lost herself in the kiss.

'Hey guys, I thought I could see the chiminea on. Woops, sorry, didn't mean to interrupt.'

On hearing Pippa's voice, Naomi wrenched herself away from Toren's body, a gush of cold air filling the void between them.

'Pip, you're back early,' he said. 'All OK?'

'Michael got called out. That's the problem with dating a copper. Too busy saving the world to wine and dine their dates.' She folded her arms and rolled her eyes in mock disgust. 'Anyway, seems like you two are having a good evening. Don't let me get in your way. I'm heading up to bed anyway.'

'Oh, no. No need. I need to get going.' Naomi flung off her blanket, and jumped from her seat.

'O-kay,' Pippa said, and shot Toren a confused look. 'Well, I'm turning in anyway. Great to see you, Naomi. Good night.'

'Night,' she and Toren answered in unison, before Pippa tactfully made herself scarce.

Naomi didn't dare look at Toren. She just headed straight for the French doors back to the house. She felt a need to fill the awkward silence that had descended, and her mouth began to work faster than her brain, resulting in a stream of discourse. 'Thanks so much for dinner. I'll call you in a few weeks once I've had chance to go through the files, and we can work out next steps.

Maybe we can do our next meeting remotely, perhaps by Skype or in a telecon.'

'Naomi . . . '

'Yes, that's probably the best thing. A telecon. I'll get my secretary to contact yours, and we can organise a time that's mutually convenient.'

'Naomi . . . '

'It's difficult to say at this stage when it will be. Maybe Tuesday. No, not Tuesday. I'm in court all day. Wednesday might be better.'

'NAOMI!'

She couldn't ignore him any longer when he raised his voice like that. She stopped to look at him, her hand poised on the door handle. 'What, Toren? What? What do you expect me to say? You're my client, and we kissed. That shouldn't happen. It can't be happening.' She drove a hand hard through her hair. It pulled, but she didn't care. She needed to feel pain; needed to wake up to the severity of the situation, and stop playing around.

'Yes, I kissed you. But you didn't seem to be objecting. In fact, I'd say you enjoyed it as much as I did, which was a lot if you hadn't noticed.'

'Oh God.' She had to work hard to resist the temptation to drop to her knees, and burst into wracks of resigned sobs. She'd spent years of her life fighting, fighting to get her life back together after he left, and now she found herself with an even bigger battle on her hands — to stop herself falling for him all over again. She should have refused to take on this case. She should have refused to work with him, insisted that Piers took it on. 'I'm such a total idiot.'

She didn't even know she'd said the words out loud, or notice he'd got up from his chair and come towards her, until she felt his hands firmly grasp her upper arms. He gave her a gentle shake that made her look up at him.

'For the record, Naomi, I never stopped loving you.'

She couldn't stop the sob now. It forced its way out of her throat, and she looked back down at the floor. He shook her gently again, and she dragged her head up to look at him again.

'But I can't let that — and the mistakes I made 10 years ago — get in the way of this case,' he added.

A single tear slipped down her cheek. She didn't even try to wipe it away. She wanted him to see her at her ugliest to keep him as far away as possible.

'I'm sorry,' he continued. 'I shouldn't have kissed you. It was unprofessional at best, tactless at worst. I let my feelings for you get in the way of my common sense. If anyone's an idiot, it's me. You have my word it won't happen again.'

Her heart plummeted to the pit of her stomach. He'd said he loved her, but in the next breath he'd made it clear she was second best to his daughter — to this case. That's the way it should be. Children came first, of course they did. Not that she could ever possibly hope to understand, since she'd never have one.

'Please don't change your mind about representing me.'

She gave a sardonic laugh. That's all he cared about. Like hell he loves me. He just doesn't want me to drop his case.

'I told you. I've committed. Unlike some people, when I make a promise, I stick to it.'

His face fell, and he released his grip on her. She meant for the words to hurt, and quite obviously they had. So why did his expression make her feel like the biggest cow on earth?

She pulled free from the loose hold he had on her, opened the door, and stalked through the house, stopping only to pick up her handbag. She flung open her car door and practically threw herself into the driver's seat. She turned on the ignition, and smacked the steering wheel with flat hands over and over again. 'You bloody stupid idiot woman! Why did you let that happen? Why, why, why, why?' She lowered her head onto the steering wheel and let out a strangled scream. 'Stupid woman,' she said, again, and gripped the wheel so hard her fingers hurt.

If she had any sense, she'd march back in there and tell him she'd changed her mind, and was handing the case over to a colleague after all. It would be for the best. But she didn't have the energy to confront him again. And despite everything, she couldn't bear seeing that look of utter desperation on his face again she'd witnessed tonight. He was relying on her.

She hated him, God, she hated him so much, but for some ridiculous reason she couldn't bring herself to let him down. The only scrap of dignity she had left was based on how good she was at her job. She wasn't prepared to lose that too. Slowly, determinedly, she raised her head, and stared out of the windscreen through a blur of tears. 'Show him, Naomi. Show him what you're made of. Show the world.' She sniffed, put the Mercedes in gear, and roared down the street.

10

'Ta-dah!' Ali whipped open the curtain on the changing room and twirled, the skirt of the gold and white dress splaying out around her.

'You look beautiful, pumpkin.' The chair next to where Toren had been standing outside the changing room for the last 45 minutes became free, and he suppressed the temptation to let out an audible 'Ahh' as he sank into it. 'So, have you decided which one you'd like?'

'Not yet. I've still got the orange one and the pink one left to try.'

'You know, sweetheart, you don't have to decide right now. It's only September. You've got three months until the school Christmas disco.'

She stopped scrutinising the two dresses she held up in her hands, and scowled at him. 'Daddy,' she said, as if about to explain something very complex to someone very simple. 'A stitch in time saves nine, that's what Pippa says.'

He smiled at her use of the phrase.

'It's important to get organised ahead of schedule, Daddy, then we don't have to stress about it nearer the time.'

'I see,' he said. 'Yes, I suppose you're right. Please carry on then, and I'll wait here until you decide.'

'Do you need coffee, is that what it is?' She put her hands on her hips in a diva-like fashion. 'There's a café across the road. I'm fine here on my own if you want to go get yourself one.'

Toren laughed at her intuitiveness. He'd have to work on reducing his caffeine intake if his nine-year-old had started to notice. 'No, no, that's fine sweetheart. I'm sure I'll survive until we've finished here.'

'Do you prefer the gold one or the pink one, Dad? Or how about the black?' His daughter had lost interest in ensuring he was entertained, and turned her attentions back to the dresses.

'Erm, well, they're all very pretty, pumpkin. Why don't you just get all of them.'

She looked at him and cocked an eyebrow.

'No, Daddy,' she hissed, peering round the curtain to see if anyone else was listening. Once she realised they were alone in the changing room area she restored her normal speaking volume. 'The other girls at school would only be allowed one dress for the Christmas disco. I don't want to grow up spoiled. One dress is fine. Besides, I can only wear one at once!'

She was right of course, and he was glad Ali had her feet firmly on the ground despite being brought up surrounded by so much wealth. He usually did his best to keep life as modest as possible for her, but the truth was, he would have bought out the whole chain of this retail store just to get out of here. As much as he adored his daughter and would do anything for her, the stuffy, brightly-lit environment of women's clothing stores pushed that resolved to the limit.

Lost in his thoughts, he didn't quite catch what Ali said next, but couldn't miss how her mouth had turned down and she was looking at the floor, shuffling her feet.

'Sorry, sweetheart, what was that?'

'I said I might not be able to go to the disco anyway.'

'Why not?'

'I might not be living with you then.'

Toren widened his eyes, his heart racing. Did she know? He worked hard at keeping his voice calm and level. 'What do you mean?'

She played with the edge of the curtain, and kept her eyes to the floor. 'If I get sent away.'

Toren jumped up from the chair, went over to Ali, and knelt down in front of her, so she had no choice but to look at him. 'What are you talking about? No-one's sending you away.'

'You don't have to pretend, Dad. I know about my mum wanting me to live with her. I know that's why you've asked Naomi to help us.'

He looked at his daughter, and for the first time since she was born she didn't look to him like a little girl. Instead, he saw the young woman she would one day be. His mind raced. Should he try to put her mind at rest, tell her she had nothing to worry about? Or was it time to be honest?

His shoulders fell, and he did the only thing he could. He wrapped his arms around her little body, and squeezed her to him, burying his face into her strawberry-smelling hair. 'You're a very clever girl, Ali, and I won't lie to you. You're right. Your mother does want you to live with her.' He released her, and held her in front of him. 'But I don't want you to worry about anything. Naomi is excellent at her job.'

Ali continued to stare at him, her face unmoving. An unpleasant sensation, like severe pins and needles, started at the top of Toren's head and travelled all the way down his body. It had never occurred to him before that she might want to live with Michelle. It wouldn't be long before she became a teenager. Perhaps she felt she needed her mother. He summoned up every scrap of humility he could to say his next words.

'Ali, do you want to go and live with your mum?'

Her eyes welled up, and tears began to spill over onto her cheeks.

'It's okay to say yes, pumpkin, if that's how you feel. I will understand.' He could say he understood, would do his best to pretend, but it would never, ever be fine with him to say goodbye to his daughter. The only way he would even so much as consider letting her go was is if it was the right thing by her.

She shook her head vehemently from side to side, a string of snot flying out of her nostril as she did. 'No, Daddy.' She clutched the arms of his sweater, her face folded into a pained expression, and the young woman who had flashed in front of him, returned to being a child. 'I don't know her. She didn't want me when I was a baby, so why does she want me?'

He searched his mind for an answer suitable for a nine-year-old. Despite his opinion of Michelle, he'd never criticised her in front of Ali. That wouldn't be fair. 'I don't know,' he admitted. He was normally the one with all the answers, and felt uncharacteristically powerless at not being able to provide one to his daughter when she needed him more than ever to give her reassurance. He pulled her tightly back into him.

She pressed her face into his chest and sobbed. 'I want to stay with you, Daddy. Please don't make me go, don't make me.'

The blood drained from his head, his body weakened. He sank down to his backside, his legs outstretched in front of him, and cradled Ali onto his lap. 'I promise you, you're not going anywhere, pumpkin. You're staying with me.' He stroked her hair, and hoped he hadn't made the first promise of his life he couldn't keep. He was used to being in control, the one who pulled the punches, but this, this was something different entirely. Naomi was good, but was Michelle's case so strong it was unwinnable? It wasn't like him to think like this — he always found a solution. He needed to empower Naomi, and do everything he could to make sure she secured victory. Then it occurred to him. Why didn't he think of that before? He knew what he had to do, and would make the phone call as soon as they got home.

★   ★   ★

'You're sending me where?'

'I told you, Naomi. I'm not sending you anywhere. Your client, Stirling, has requested you go to Vienna for the next six weeks to focus solely on his case.'

'How can I possibly, Richard? I'm not working with Stirling exclusively. I'm still wrapping up the Keyton-Meyer case too.' She placed her hands on her hips, and glared at Richard Chailey, one of the partners of the firm. She normally treated her boss of seven years with perfect respect, but this piece of news got under her skin so much she couldn't hold her tongue.

'I'll get someone else to draw the Keyton-Meyer case to a close for you. You've done all the hard work on that one already. It just needs someone to dot the Is and cross Ts and we'll be on the home straight.'

'Why send me away? What's wrong with London?'

'Stirling called first thing and said he was concerned your other cases were taking you away from his.'

'Typical!' she said. 'It's all about him.'

Richard raised his eyebrows, and she quickly stopped herself saying more. She didn't want him to know they had history. He could take her off the case all together, and even discipline her for getting involved when she had a personal tie to the client. She placed her hands on his highly polished desk and leaned forward. 'And you agreed to his demands without asking me first?'

'The man is offering to pay five times your usual rate. And your usual rate is as steep as it gets. You're highly sought-after, Naomi. You know you are.'

No matter how sought-after she might be, how good at her job, it didn't stop Toren from having control over her. She'd thought it was only her heart, but it was becoming clear his power even stretched to her working life too. A searing arrow of hatred for him shot through her.

'I thought you had scruples, Richard!' Taking her frustration out on her boss might not be her wisest move, but as Toren wasn't here for her to direct her anger at, it was her only option.

The normally mild-mannered Chailey

leaned forward on his side of the desk, mirroring her threatening posture. 'I have a business to run, Naomi. You command some of the highest fees in the city. Stirling is offering to multiply them five times if you work from his home in Vienna. I thought you wanted to make partner here soon.'

'I do,' she said, pensively. Toren had taken enough from her already, she'd be damned if he was going to scupper her career prospects too.

'Then surely you can see that this is an offer neither you nor I can refuse.'

She nodded slowly, accepting the opportunity to shut up.

'Besides. It's not exactly a hardship. The man is a billionaire. I don't think his Viennese bolthole will be too shoddy.'

'Why Vienna? He's got houses all over the world.'

Richard shrugged. 'Why not? Anyway, there's no time for questions. Your flight leaves at two.'

She flicked up the sleeve of her suit

jacket to expose her watch face. 'Are you kidding me? That's barely four hours away.'

Richard smiled and picked up his brief case, indicating the conversation was over. 'Best get going then, hadn't you?'

She clamped her teeth together to save herself saying something she'd regret, picked up the notepad and pen she carried everywhere, and walked out, aware her stiletto heels were clattering louder than normal on the polished wooden floor of the office.

*   *   *

'Not half bad.' Dee let out a low whistle, and lay her immaculate red leather gloves on top of the 12-seater dining room table. She did a slow full turn, taking in the whole of the room.

'Trust me, when you've been rattling around an eight-bedroom Viennese townhouse on your own for almost six weeks, it starts to lose its novelty.'

191

Dee span around to look at her, then burst out laughing. 'Listen at you, darling! You sound like a petulant child. You even look like one, all folded arms and pouty lips.'

Suddenly self-conscious, Naomi pushed herself up from against the window where she'd been leaning, and uncrossed her arms. 'I'm just saying, that being stuck here on my own . . . '

'Right bang in the centre of one of Europe's most beautiful cities? Yes, I'm listening,' cut in Dee, a twinkle in her eye.

'Well, yes, but I don't know anyone here, and I'm just working on the one case. There's not even any variety in the work, and it can get lonely.'

'I hate to say I told you so.' Dee ran a hand over the top of a purple velvet-upholstered dining chair. 'You should have turned down this case when you had the chance. As soon as Richard got a sniff of the money involved to send you here, there was no way he'd refuse.'

'Yes, I know, but I dare say Toren would have got his own way in the end, with or without Richard. He always does.' She turned to look out of the window onto a beautifully crisp October day in Stephansplatz. Despite the early hour, crowds had already started to gather at the entrance of St Stephen's Cathedral, eager to see the impressive mediaeval architecture from the inside. It was hard to really ever feel lonely when you were positioned in the very heart of Vienna. Whenever she felt she needed a dose of human company, she chose from one of the hundreds of beautiful patisseries the city offered, and sat there a while, watching the world go by.

'So, are you going to show me some of the best coffee houses this place has to offer, or am I going to stand around forever listening to you complain about your ex-husband? I am only here for two days you know.'

'Speaking of which', she grabbed the handle of Dee's designer wheelie case and gestured for her friend to follow. 'We're going to make the most of this weekend. You're my first and only visitor, and I only have one more week before I'm due back in London.' She ushered Dee into the elevator, stepped inside to join her, and pressed the button for the guest floor.

'Darling, this place is so huge it even has its own elevator. I can't believe you're so desperate to leave!'

Naomi rolled her eyes. 'I normally take the stairs. If I get stuck in this thing no-one will hear me scream.'

Dee looked at her, and reached out to give her cheek a friendly pinch. 'You poor thing,' she said. 'Getting paid five times your normal already huge salary and having to live in this hovel.'

She laughed, in spite of herself, and jokingly batted her friend's hand away. 'I just feel pushed into it, that's all.'

The elevator pinged, and both women stepped out. 'Well, I tell you something, darling,' Dee said. 'You might have a bone to pick with this man, but he's certainly got taste.'

She couldn't deny that one. Decorated in a modern take on Baroque style, the guest quarters oozed opulence, while still succeeding in looking homely and comfortable at the same time. 'Well, it's all yours for the next two nights. Want me to help you unpack?'

'Yes, but not now.' Dee buttoned her open cashmere coat back up, and linked arms with her. 'I can see you're in need of some serious retail therapy. To the shops!' Dee pointed back to the lift, and did a little gallop. Naomi laughed. She'd missed her friend, and if truth be known, Dee wasn't the only person she missed.

★   ★   ★

Naomi awoke with a gasp, her heart pounding in her chest with the speed and ferocity of a thundering racehorse. What was that? She was certain a thud close by had woken her, but now there was only silence. The noise had shaken her, and she was wide awake. She willed her eyes to become accustomed to the darkness as she desperately tried to make out the familiar shapes of the bedroom.

She hated being here, in this huge Viennese mansion all alone. She had barely slept a wink during her first week, and had flinched at every unfamiliar creak. Sheer exhaustion had brought her slumber in the end, and as the weeks went on, she got used to the natural noises of the house, but the sound that had wrenched her from sleep just now was one she'd never heard before.

All was quiet. She must have been dreaming. Her pulse began to slowly return to normal, and she released the breath she'd been holding. When she was sure she had imagined it, she allowed her eyes to close again, and let her neck relax into the pillow.

Scraaape. A different noise this time. She flung her eyes open. Her whole body froze. Someone's here. In my bedroom. She strained her ears so much they hurt. She could hear someone breathing. So close. Fight or flight? She wanted to run, to head for the door, but her body was rigid. Paralysed by fear.

Did whoever it was know she was there? Had they come to attack her, or was this an attempt at a robbery, and they thought the house was empty? There were certainly plenty of treasures in this house that thieves would love to get their hands on. Careful not to move her head, so the intruder couldn't hear her hair against the pillow, she looked as far out of the corner of her eye as she could to try and locate him. Still hoping she was imagining it all, the sight of the huge, dark male figure against the window caused a rush of cold sweat to drench her entire body.

Maybe he hadn't realised she was there. If she just stayed still, didn't make a peep or move a muscle, he might just find some cash or antiques he wanted, and make a quick getaway. She said a silent, desperate prayer, and hoped against hope he wouldn't come any closer to the bed.

He coughed, and she jumped. He wasn't even trying to keep quiet now, brazen as he was. Go away, go away, go away. The shape of him loomed bigger, and bigger as he came closer. He stretched out his arm towards the bed. He touched the cover, then lifted it.

Oh. My. God.

Her fear paralysis lifted, and pure self-protection took its place. She screamed — a roaring scream which cut her throat to shreds, but anything, anything to get him away from him. She thrashed out, clawing, slapping and scratching at him with her hands. He held his arms out in front of his body to defend himself, and he too shouted out — harsh, guttural words in German, which she didn't understand.

'No, no, get away from me, leave me alone!' She propelled herself out the opposite side of the bed, her heart racing so hard she thought it would burst out of her chest.

'Naomi!'

Oh my God. He knew her name.

She heard a snap, and her irises burned with the light that flooded the room. She shielded her eyes, whilst at the same time trying to get a glimpse of her attacker. If she survived she might at least be able to identify him afterwards.

'You!' She didn't know whether to cry with relief or scream at him for the stress he'd just put her through. 'I thought you were trying to kill me. What the hell are you doing here?' She could barely get her words out through shaking so much.

'Naomi, it's okay, just relax. No-one's going to hurt you.' Toren walked round the bed to where she stood, and enveloped her in his arms. 'I'm so sorry I frightened you.'

She collapsed against him. The warmth from his body, and the familiar scent of his expensive cologne instantly calmed her as he rocked her gently from side to side.

She took a few moments to gather herself, before raising her head to look up at him. 'Toren, what are you doing coming into my room in the middle of the night? Why were you speaking German at me?'

He ran a firm hand up and down her back to soothe her. She hated the way it felt so good. 'I didn't realise it was you. I assumed you were a local squatter. Now you're wide awake, let's go to the kitchen and get you some brandy for the shock, and I can explain every-thing.'

Her nerves still shot to pieces, she allowed him to lead her gently by the hand out of the room.

Only then did she realise how scantily clad she had been. Dressed only in cotton panties and a thigh-length strappy chemise, her outfit left little to the imagination. She said a silent thank you to God she hadn't slept naked as she sometimes did. The thought of it made her pull the neckline tighter around her.

He took her hand again and, just as she always did, he shunned the elevator in favour of the staircase.

★ ★ ★

He watched her sip the sugary tea he'd made her, no doubt bitter from the addition of a generous glug of brandy, and saw her shoulders drop several inches from around her ears as she swallowed.

'Is it helping?' He wiped away the remnants of his tea-making from the kitchen counter, and tried to avert his gaze from her gaping dressing gown. She'd looked so vulnerable in the bedroom when she'd mistaken him for an intruder, that for the first time since ordering her boss to send her to Vienna, he regretted the decision. She must be so lonely here, so isolated. He breathed in and forced the thought away. She was a grown woman. She could handle

201

herself. He had to focus on what was best for his daughter — what gave him the best chance of winning the case. Sending Naomi here had been the best thing to do. For everyone.

'Getting there, thanks.'

'Naomi, I really didn't mean to scare you. I didn't know you were there.'

'You were the one who sent me here.' She had allowed him to lead her downstairs, had obediently sipped the drink he'd made her, but now her fear was subsiding and normal logic returning, he could almost see the jigsaw pieces reforming in her brain. Her eyes narrowed. She was angry with him all right. Angry he'd sent her here several weeks ago on a whim after offering her boss an absurd amount of money to have him work exclusively on his case.

'I thought you'd be in the master bedroom as I'd suggested in my email. It's a much bigger room. Why weren't you in there?'

She shrugged. 'I preferred the other room. It's smaller and cosier. I don't need all that space just for me. Anyway, the point is why are you here at all? I'm due home in two days' time. You could have seen me then.'

It was his turn to shrug. 'I thought I'd accompany you on the journey home. It will give us an opportunity to catch up on where you've got to with the case.'

She looked from left to right, as if registering the information, and he braced himself. She wasn't going to let him get off that lightly.

'Toren, after persuading Richard Chailey to exile me out here, we haven't spoken once. All our communication has been through email, and pretty perfunctory at that.'

'Have I been cooperative enough?' He flung the dishcloth into the sink, and furrowed his brow, concerned he hadn't done everything in his power to provide her with all the tools she needed to help him keep Ali.

'Cooperative? Completely. You've answered my questions regarding the case, and provided me with any materials I've requested straight away. But you've never once answered the one question I repeatedly ask you.'

He hooked his thumbs over the pockets of his jeans and raised his eyebrows. He knew exactly what she meant, but the only strategy he could think of at such short notice was to feign ignorance.

She widened her eyes and leaned forward, as if explaining to an idiot. 'Why you felt the need to send me to Vienna. Get me to work exclusively on your case, fine, but why couldn't I have done that from London?'

He picked his coffee cup up by the rim, and went to sit beside her. 'I didn't want you to have any distractions'. He sipped his drink, and wiped his brow with the back of his bare forearm. He'd never minded confrontation in his work, or in any other walk of life for that matter, but he had acted inexcusably in banishing her abroad to work solely for him with barely any notice.

He told himself over and over he had no choice under the circumstances. It's for Ali. Anything for Ali.

He took another, longer gulp to buy himself thinking time. The scalding liquid burnt the roof of his mouth, and he winced. Something told him he deserved the pain. 'I wanted you to focus on the case. And I wanted to focus on my daughter, not get side-lined.'

He looked at her out of the corner of his eye, and she quickly looked away. It didn't take a genius to work out that was code for her being a distraction for him. 'I want to spend as much time as possible with my daughter. While I still can.'

'I see.'

He couldn't decipher her tone. Was it understanding laced with sadness, or resentment? He sighed. In trying to do the right thing by everyone, he'd ended up causing her — and him, based on how he'd felt without her for the past six weeks — even more pain and heartache.

'Why didn't you let me know you were coming? I know it's your house and all, but it would have been good to get some sort of notice you were going to turn up in the middle of night, rather than frighten me to death.'

'I thought if I told you I was planning to come, you might cut your stay short, and return to London early.'

'So, what if I had? You would have caught up with me back home, no doubt.'

He licked his lips. This wasn't a conversation he'd been planning on having until tomorrow. He was going to greet her in a civilised fashion in the morning, not scare the living daylights out of her at two in the morning. Only once he'd filled her stomach with one of his trademark cooked breakfasts was he going to broach the subject of the ball.

'I've pulled a few strings and got tickets to the Viennese doctors' ball tomorrow night.'

She knitted her brow, and was silent

for a few seconds, before realisation fell over her face.

'Woah, woah.' She shook her head, furiously. 'Let me guess. Michelle's new surgeon husband will be there, and you want to check him out? No, Toren, no way. You can't do that. It will look bad to the judge if you're found to be stalking the opposing party ahead of the hearing.' She sat up straighter, transforming before his eyes from defenceless female to the high-powered attorney she was.

'Not exactly,' he said. 'I have it on good authority that he won't be in attendance.'

'Then, why are you going?' She stared at him, unblinking, as if paragraphs away from reaching the conclusion of a thriller novel.

'Because plenty of his colleagues will be there.'

'Oh no, Toren.' She pulled her hair away from her face, and glared at him, wide-eyed. 'Please, take my advice as your lawyer. Don't even think about it.

You could severely jeopardise your chances of securing victory in this case if you turn up at that ball tomorrow.'

He held out a hand to calm her. 'They'll have no idea who I am. I'm just going to keep my ear to the ground. If I overhear a snippet of a conversation that could discredit him, then so be it. If not, then it will be nothing other than an enjoyable evening out.'

She drained the contents of her cup and stuck out her tongue at the bitter taste of the alcohol. 'Won't you look out of place? Surely couples go to a ball to dance together. You're going to look fairly conspicuous as a man on his own trying to eavesdrop into people's conversations.

He held her gaze until the penny dropped. She shook her head rapidly, and waved a finger from side to side. 'Oh, no, no, no, no, no. No way. There's no way you're dragging me into this . . . this subterfuge. Anyway, I've got two left feet. With you earwigging and me standing on everyone's toes, your cover will be blown in no time. No chance. Forget it. You're insane. Goodnight.'

She placed her hands flat on the table and used them to push herself up from her chair. She was still shaking her head and mumbling something about him being totally crazy as she reached the kitchen door.

'Oh, Naomi, there is one more thing.'

She paused, and turned to look back at him. Her face was sombre, and for a moment he considered not embroiling her into his plans. But then Ali's face flashed in front of his eyes, and he pushed away the guilt. He was doing this for his little girl. He reached into his back pocket and produced two cream and gold tickets. 'I've already cleared your attendance at the ball with Richard Chailey. He said he was sure you'd be most enthusiastic about the invitation. He also said he'd been very impressed with the way you've handled this case so far, and wants to speak to you when you're back in London.

Something about you becoming a partner.'

She pressed her lips together tightly, and her cheekbones sharpened. That was a fed-up look if ever he'd seen one.

'You really are something, Toren,' she said quietly. 'As if it weren't enough to have me sent here without discussing it with me first, you're now organising my social engagements for me through my employer.'

He stood up, and shoved the tickets back into his jeans pocket. 'You know why I'm doing all this, Naomi. I can't face losing her. I love Ali with all my heart, and I'll do everything I can to keep her.'

He could have been mistaken, but he thought for a fleeting second her face softened. She smoothed her sleek, cropped hair behind her ear, and relaxed her mouth, parting her lips slightly. 'I have nothing to wear for a ball.'

'Yes, you do.'

She raised her eyebrows as if he'd

gone completely mad.

'In the dressing room wardrobe. I bought it for you. It should be a good fit. I hope you like it.'

Going behind people's backs to get his own way wasn't his usual style, but he was prepared to resort to every necessary below-the-belt tactic to keep his daughter. He only hoped that in her heart Naomi could find some under-standing for why he was behaving as he was.

She stared at him, open-mouthed and gave a short, exasperated laugh.

He wasn't going to stand around to hear her thoughts on his revelation. As she no longer appeared to be in a hurry to go back to bed, he took the opportunity to go first, hesitating only momentarily on his way passed her, by giving her a quick kiss on the cheek. Perhaps she'd see it as it was intended — a silent form of apology.

11

Naomi wrapped a towel around her damp body, and stepped out of the en suite bathroom, into the bedroom. She paused as she saw a flash of white on top of the bed. The note hadn't been there 10 minutes ago when she'd thrown off her clothes and headed for the shower. She'd been so desperate to wash away some of the anger her early morning exchange with Toren had built up, she hadn't cared where she discarded them.

She recognised his jagged handwriting from where she stood, but couldn't make out the content. More demands, probably. She walked over to the bed, and snatched up the note.

Naomi,
There are things I have to do today. I'll meet you at the Kursalon

for the ball. Your driver will arrive here 8pm sharp to pick you up. You should find everything you need in the wardrobe.

Toren.

With a scream of frustration, she crumpled the paper into a ball and threw it into the waste bin by the bed. The arrogance of the man! She stomped over to the wardrobe, chuntering to herself about his unreasonable expectations. 'He thinks he can march back into my life and start telling me what to do, where to work, even what to damn well wear!'

She flung open the wardrobe doors, and what she saw brought her verbal tirade to an immediate halt. There, right in front of her, was the most exquisite dress she'd ever seen. Full-length, ivory and silk, it was reminiscent of a 1920s ball gown. She lifted it from the hanger and held it in front of her. Despite the ornate bronze detailing on the straps and lower back, it was surprisingly light. The quality of the seam work was impeccable. It couldn't possibly fit though. How could it? He'd never asked for her measurements.

She shook off her towel, and stepped into the dress. She held her breath, and waited for the moment the fabric refused to be pulled any further up her body because it was too small. To her surprise, it slid over her hips easily, past her waist, and over her breasts. Finally, she hooked her arms through the bronze-encrusted straps, and pulled up the side zip. It's bound to gape, she thought, knowing how difficult it was to get slim-fitting dresses to flatter her athletic shape.

She closed the wardrobe, and saw herself in the full-length mirror, which hung on the front of the door. She gulped. Not only did it fit like a glove, but it was her dream dress. When they'd got married money had been tight. Using her basic sewing skills, she'd adapted her mum's old wedding dress. Toren had told her how ravishing she looked, but still it wasn't hers. It wasn't her dream dress. When he slipped it from her shoulders on their wedding night, and held her close, she'd whispered in his ear. She told him to close his eyes, and described to him how she had wanted to look for him on their wedding day.

Her eyes filled with tears as she recalled her words. It's long, ivory and silk, like something a 1920s screen goddess would wear. It's completely backless, and where the fabric gathers at my waist it has the most beautiful bronze jewels you've ever seen.

He'd remembered. She looked down at the cowl neck, and the way the darts at the waist skimmed her body, and flattered her figure. This was no off-the-shelf gown. He'd had it tailor-made. For her. But what was she supposed to wear with it? She thought back to his note. You'll find everything you need in the wardrobe.

She clicked open the wardrobe door again, and saw two boxes on a low shelf. One was a shoe box, and the other was smaller, royal blue and covered with velvet.

She lifted both out and carried them to the bed, where she sat and explored the contents. The shoes matched the gown beautifully. They were ivory satin, bejewelled in bronze, and with a dainty buckle T-bar. Despite the height of the heel, they were the most comfortable shoes she'd ever worn. Her bare feet would have sighed with pleasure if they could when she slipped them on.

'Oh, Toren,' she said, to the empty room, as she lifted the lid of the velvet box to reveal a three-tier platinum and diamond necklace and drop earrings, which matched the embellishments on the dress to perfection. She clipped on the earrings, and secured the necklace around her neck, then stood up, held the front part of her hair back, and faced the mirror. The beautiful bride she'd dreamed of being stared back at her. She'd heard other women say they felt like a princess when they wore their fantasy dress on their wedding day. She'd always scoffed at the idea — prided herself on having her feet on the ground more than they did. Now for the first time, she understood what they meant.

The sight of Toren's tormented face flashed in front of her eyes, and his earlier words floated into her consciousness — 'I can't face losing her. I love Ali with all my heart, and I'll do everything I can to keep her.'

She let her hair fall back down and, feeling guilty, looked over at the bin where the screwed-up note lay. He was doing all this to save his little girl, while all she could do was complain — complain to her boss for paying her more money than most people could ever dream of earning, and complain to her best friend that she had to spend seven weeks in Toren's luxurious Viennese mansion. Despite everything Toren was going through, he'd remembered her words to him on their wedding day, and bought her the most perfect dress she'd ever worn.

Never had she looked so beautiful but felt so ugly inside.

★　★　★

From the moment he saw the high-heeled shoe emerge from behind the car door Toren couldn't pull his gaze away. His driver offered a white-gloved hand to the woman in the back of the limousine. She took it, and stepped elegantly out.

He sucked his breath in, and by the way the gathering crowd outside the Kursalon silenced and every man turned their head to look at her, he knew he wasn't the only one. He'd commissioned one of London's top designers to make the dress. It had cost a small fortune, but he would have paid 10 times the price to see her in the gown she coveted. She looked glowing, angelic and so very comfortable in her own skin.

She turned her head from side to

side, a coy smile on her lips. She hadn't spotted him yet. He strode over to her, and was the proudest man on earth to offer her his arm. 'Shall we?'

She beamed, and her shimmery lipstick caught the light streaming out from the roof of the Kursalon. 'Yes.' She hooked her hand into the crook of her arm. She laughed lightly, and her bright eyes creased at the corners. 'Lets.'

The transformation in her from this morning when they'd argued in his kitchen was palpable. Optimism swelled in his chest. She was happy. He realised with a pang what he wanted more than anything in the world was to make his girls happy forever. His girls. Ali and Naomi.

He led her into the impressive ballroom, where grand chandeliers glinted overhead. He felt her pull back, and he led her gently to a corner of the room. Women in sparkling ball gowns and their gentlemen partners in tailed dinner jackets swirled around the black and white dance floor in time to the upbeat classical music. He cast a sideways glance at her, and saw her eyes were wide in wonder and more than a hint of trepidation.

'It's the Viennese Waltz.' He stroked her hand to reassure her the situation wasn't foreign to him, and she needn't be nervous. 'Want to give it a go?'

She shook her head vehemently, causing the drop earrings he'd had made for her to swing from side to side.

He laughed and gave her fingers a squeeze. 'Okay, let's get a drink first.' He winked at a waitress nearby who was carrying a tray of champagne glasses. She came over, and smiled at him, proffering the tray. 'Danke schoen.' He unwound his arm from Naomi's and took two glasses. The waitress returned his wink, then disappeared into the crowds, shooting him several backward glances as she went.

'Prost.' He offered one of the glasses to Naomi. She accepted it, and took several sips.

'Presumably you're not expecting me to dance? You know what terrible balance I have.'

He laughed, recalling the few occasions he'd witnessed her take to the dance floor. 'Don't worry.' He slipped his arm around her waist, and rested his hand on the smooth flesh of her exposed back. 'The man always leads in ballroom dancing.'

'That might be more reassuring,' she said. 'If I knew how to follow.'

He leaned in and spoke into her ear, so she could hear him above the music. 'Just relax, and let my body guide yours. That's the secret.'

She nodded and sipped her drink several times more. Her eyes darting from side to side as couples span around and around only feet away. 'I thought you wanted to eavesdrop on a few conversations rather than spend the evening dancing. Wasn't that the whole point of being here tonight? I was to act as a ruse, and you were to find out the dirt on Michelle's new husband?'

The orchestra reached a crescendo and the piece came to an end. The dancers paused on the floor, and turned to the stage to applaud.

'Later.' He took her glass, and placed it on a nearby table, then took her by the hand and pulled her through the throng of dancers to the centre of the floor.

'Oh, Toren, no. I'm going to need a few more of those glasses of champagne before I even so much as think about taking to the dancefloor. Go and dance with someone who actually knows what they're doing. I'll just embarrass myself — and you for that matter.'

He ignored her protests and took her in a classic ballroom hold, with his left hand clasping her right. He pulled her into his body by placing his other hand on the small of her back. The band started up again. The violinists moved their bows so fast against their strings that their elbows seemed in danger of flying out of control.

One, two, three, one, two, three. He

guided her round, then round again, and again, until everything was a blur apart from her face, which remained in perfect clarity. Several seconds into the dance, and her body began to relax into his. For the first time ever, they were truly dancing together. They'd attempted it a few times during their marriage, but it had never really gelled. But now, it was all falling into place.

Her lips stretched into a natural smile. She felt the synergy of their bodies too. He could tell by the sparkle in her emerald eyes, and the glow of her cheeks.

Together they span around the floor. Having been to many a Viennese ball over the last decade, he was a practiced dancer, but even he had never experienced this sensation of floating before. Somehow everything worked. Their bodies melded together as one, flying across the sprung floor as if they were dancing on clouds. Their feet seemed to be inexplicably linked to each other's, and moved in perfect synchronisation to the beat of the uplifting classical rhythms. And never did they break eye contact. The dance floor was packed, and Toren should have been constantly monitoring for a space to guide them both into, but it was as if they were in an impenetrable bubble, which other couples moved aside for.

He couldn't temper his facial muscles, which were stretched from one ear to the other. He knew he was grinning like an idiot, but the feel of her soft body against him combined with the up-tempo music and the exhilaration of swirling round and round the floor like a pair of teenagers brought that surge of optimism shooting through his body again, but this time threefold what it had been earlier. In that very moment, that very second, he felt he could die of happiness.

Much too soon the music stopped. She released herself from his hold, and turned to applaud the band. He was aware he was clapping his hands along with everyone else, but instead of facing the stage, he remained rooted to the spot, taking in her profile. She wore her short hair swept away from her face, leaving her forehead exposed, and he noticed how a faint sheen of perspiration glowed under the light from the grand chandelier overhead. The tip of her slightly pointed nose caught a glint too, creating a mischievous look, which was almost elfin-like.

The lead musician addressed the crowd in German. 'They're taking down the tempo now with a slow waltz,' Toren translated for her.

She looked from side to side at the couples surrounding them. The men were drawing their partners into an intimate hold, and many were cheek-to-cheek. Her wide smile gradually faded. She wrung her hands together and let them fall to below her stomach. 'Time to get a drink then, I suppose,' she said, avoiding his eyes.

Make this easy for yourself, and just agree. Despite his inner dialogue telling him not to go there, he found himself taking a step towards her. 'Not yet.' He clasped her right hand in his left, and raised it up to dance hold. '*Come Waltz With Me* is one of my favourite songs to dance to.' She looked up at him, her green eyes shining, but said nothing. Did I realise when we were together just how beautiful those eyes were?

He laid his other hand on the small of her back, and pulled her to him until their abdomens pressed against each other. They were so close her hair tickled his chin. Slowly, he began to move in time to the music, leading her through the steps.

The singer crooned the lyrics about a couple who danced together one last time before parting company. Toren had always loved those lyrics, but never had they seemed so pertinent as tonight. He pulled Naomi a little closer to him, held her hand a little tighter. For the first time since he'd stepped foot in her office several weeks before, it occurred to him that once the court case was over, he'd have no cause to see her again. Not that she wanted to, anyway. She'd made that crystal clear.

Trusting his senses to guide them both safely around the floor, he closed his eyes. If this was going to be the last time he held her, felt her, smelled her, he wanted to savour it. He wanted to remember how her skin felt beneath his palm, how her sweet scent threatened to weaken him when he breathed her in.

The song finished. He opened his eyes, and glanced down at her. She lifted her head and met his gaze. This time neither broke away as the band was applauded — they just held each other close, as if both were scared to break the spell if they took even the smallest step away. The music started up again. Neither spoke. He took the liberty to lead her into the next dance, and she let him.

Song after song they danced, and as the music once again lifted in tempo, so did the speed of their steps. She trod on his feet several times during an energetic pasa doble, and on those of a few nearby dancers when she attempted a spin in the rumba, but as the night went on, her inhibitions disappeared, and her wide smile dazzled brighter. When he lowered her into a particularly ambitious dip to mark the end of a tango number. She squealed in delight like a young girl, and when he lifted her back to standing she threw her head back and laughed.

'That's it!' She let go of him and placed her hands on her hips. Her chest moved up and down as she got her breath back, and she placed a hand on the neckline of her dress to indicate how hard her heart was beating. 'I need a break. And, I need a drink!' She reached out and tapped his upper arm. 'Come on, let's go to the bar. This one's on me, as a thank you for making me look half decent on a dancefloor — something I've never managed to achieve before.'

He placed a hand between her

shoulder blades and guided her through the throngs of dancers to the bar. 'Nothing to do with me. You held your own out there.'

She rested her elbows on the bar, and turned her head to look at him beside her, her eyebrows raised. 'Do you think?'

He screwed his lips, as if contemplating. 'Well, you did nearly break my arm in that spin, but apart from that, you made Ginger Rogers look like she had two left feet.'

'Oh, sorry about that. Must have got carried away.'

He shook his head to show he was exaggerating and grinned. She tapped him playfully on his arm in protest at his joke, and he pouted and rubbed the area her hand had been. 'Careful. That's the one you broke.'

She rolled her eyes, then leaned in to place her order. The barman poured two glasses of champagne. She thanked him, picked them up by the stems, and handed one to Toren.

'Zum Wohl,' he said, raising his glass to her.

'Tsum Tsool,' she mistakenly pronounced back.

He smiled. 'Good job you're a whizz at law, because your language skills are second only to your dancing.'

She struggled to swallow the mouthful of liquid in her mouth through the urge to laugh, and pressed a hand flat against her lips. 'Well, at least I try on both scores,' she said, once she'd finally managed to send the champagne safely down her food pipe rather than spray it all over him.

'You certainly do, Naomi, and that's what I love about you.'

The words slipped from his lips before he'd had chance to think through the magnitude of their meaning. She stopped laughing abruptly. Then she smiled, the apples of her cheeks shining with happiness and perspiration. He breathed an internal sigh of relief that she'd recognise his choice of words as a turn of phrase.

'Naomi, I know you didn't choose to come here this evening, and believe me, I can completely understand why, but I want you to know that I'm very grateful you came. Not least because I am having the most fantastic evening.'

To his surprise, she lay her hand on his forearm, which was resting on the bar.

'I'm glad I came too. I didn't think for one second I was going to enjoy tonight, but what can I say — I'm actually loving it. Thank you.'

'Thank you. For everything. For coming here with me tonight, for agreeing to work with me, for putting up with my demands that you work from my home in Vienna. I appreciate all of it. I appreciate you.'

He inched towards her, and he could have sworn she did the same. He reached his other arm around her, and traced his fingertips over the now clammy bare flesh the back of her dress exposed. They were milliseconds away from kissing — so close her breath warmed his lips.

'Well, well, what do we have here? It's the Stirling lovebirds. Long time, no see.' A firm slap on Toren's back almost sent him off balance. If it weren't for Naomi's quick reflexes at moving quickly back, he might have headbutted her.

The man's hair was thinner, and his middle even portlier than 10 years ago, but Toren recognised him immediately as their neighbour from when they'd lived in their marital home. 'Steve McBride? Good to see you again after all these years. What are you doing here?' He shook Steve's hand firmly, keeping his other arm around Naomi.

McBride swayed slightly on his feet, no doubt due to the amount of alcohol he'd consumed. He always had liked a drink. 'Hey, this is the medics ball, right? Have you forgotten what I do for a living, Stirling?' McBride burst into laughter, causing his jowls and belly to jiggle simultaneously.

'Oh right, yes, of course.' How could

he forget? He'd spent the six months they lived next door to each other avoiding getting into conversation with the self-important hospital administrator. He and Naomi had been relieved when McBride had sold up, even though on the run up to him leaving, it had meant putting up with several blow by blow accounts of his new four-storey West End townhouse.

McBride slapped Toren's upper arm over-enthusiastically as if they were sharing the best joke in the world. Finally, his laughter subsided, although his cheeks had become so red they were almost purple.

'And look at this.' McBride swept his eyes up and down Naomi like she were a piece of tasty meat he couldn't wait to get his chops around. He looked up at Toren, and nudged him conspiratorially with his elbow. 'Age hasn't done her any harm, has it? You're a lucky git, you are, Stirling.'

Toren smiled down at McBride, masking his desire to punch him between the eyes. He couldn't stand men who spoke to women as if they weren't there, but starting a fight would ruin everyone's night. He stretched a territorial arm further around Naomi's waist, and pulled her closer towards him. She rubbed her hand up and down his back, which he knew was her way of telling him not to react.

'Yeah, you're right. I am so lucky. Enjoy the rest of your evening.' He turned his body towards Naomi, signalling to McBride their conversation was over, but in his half-drunk state, McBride didn't get the hint.

'So, still live in the old street, do you? Nah, you can't. You two must've moved up in the world by now. Bet you've got a football team of kids now. Probably need at least five bedrooms to house them all. Those modern builds we used to live in were smart enough, just had thin walls, didn't they? You two newly-weds used to keep me up all night, you did.'

Toren clenched his jaw as McBride's

podgy elbow poked once again into his bicep. He turned to him, ready to tell him in no uncertain terms where to go, only to find their unwelcome visitor bent over double in another fit of laughter.

Beneath his arm he felt Naomi's shoulders sag. He raised his hand up to the back of her neck, and squeezed it gently in an attempt to ease her pain at what she'd just had to listen to. Moments ago they'd been sharing a dazzling evening together, and had been on the verge of kissing. Now the magic of the night was shattered.

'Although I tell you what, Stirling . . . ' McBride's words cut into Toren's dismal thoughts. 'Childbirth must agree with your wife. She's even more gorgeous than I remember. Don't let that one get away, will you?'

Toren's self-regulating switch flipped over in his head. In less than one second he'd let go of Naomi, and grabbed McBride by his bow tie. 'Listen you cretinous man,' he seethed through clenched teeth. 'Disrespect me or my wife again, and you'll be the one begging to get away. Now get lost.' He flicked his wrist to release him, and McBride stumbled backwards.

McBride managed to steady himself, and avoid tumbling to the floor. 'No need for that, Stirling. I was only trying to be friendly.' He hastily stuffed his shirt back inside his trouser waistband. 'Too bad your ego gets in the way of your sense of humour.'

Toren stepped towards McBride, who quickly scuttled away, the back of his shirt still dangling over the top of his trousers like a fat white tail.

He rubbed his forehead. 'Sorry about him. Are you okay?' He turned back to Naomi only to find an empty space at the bar where she'd been stood. He looked from left to right. A few ball guests stared back. His minor fracas with McBride had obviously attracted their attention. He looked around for any sign of Naomi, but she had gone.

12

Her toes screamed in pain after all the dancing, and the pavement was wet and slippery, but still she walked as fast as her legs would carry her. A large group of excited revellers passed her shouting and laughing. She kept her head down, so they didn't notice her face, which must by now be streaked in mascara from the rain and her tears.

'Naomi, wait!' Toren sounded far enough away that she could turn into the next alleyway without him seeing. The last party-goer in the crowd skipped past her, and she lifted her head back up to better see where she was heading. The light from the lamp-posts blurred in an orange stream in her tear-fuzzed vision.

'Naomi!'

He was getting closer. She picked up her pace even more, and darted into a narrow alleyway. She didn't know how safe this part of the city was for a lone woman, but she'd take her chances rather than face Toren after that excruciating experience at the ball with Steve McBride. People could be so disgustingly insensitive.

She pressed her back against the wall, forgetting her dress was completely backless, and she'd been far too upset to retrieve her coat from cloakroom. The freezing, jagged stone behind her was a sharp reminder as it cut into her exposed flesh. Her reflex cry of pain couldn't have been more poorly timed. A tall, dark figure running past the alleyway stopped so abruptly upon hearing it that he skidded to a halt and almost lost his balance.

'Naomi. Are you all right?'

His handsome face was etched with concern, as he came close to her, and looked her over, checking for any signs she was hurt.'

'Please, Toren, just leave me alone. I don't want to talk about it. I should never have come tonight.'

He placed a tender hand on her upper arm. 'You're freezing, and drenched.' He stripped off his dinner jacket and wrapped it around her.

His kindness unlocked the emotions she'd been fighting to keep in, and she collapsed into sobs. 'That idiot Steve McBride . . . what he said . . . it, it, brought it all back.'

He wrapped his arms around her and pulled her into him. His shirt was cold and wet against her cheek, but the heat from his body warmed her through. He stroked a dripping strand of hair away from her face, and uttered something soothing and comforting into her ear, but his words were drowned out by the blood rushing through her head as she tried to quell her crying.

'Don't let McBride get to you. He's an idiot all right, but he's also an idiot who didn't know we'd separated, or that we couldn't have children. We can't blame him for that.'

'I know, I know.' Her words were

muffled against his body. 'It's just that what he said hurt so much because it's what should have happened. He confronted me with what my life should have been like had my body not failed me. Or should I say, failed us.'

He placed his hands gently on the sides of her face, and tipped it up to meet his. 'Stop that. Stop that right now. You were the best wife. The best wife ever. And I loved you. You couldn't have let me down if you tried.'

She blinked against the fat raindrops, which rudely fell on her face as she brought him into focus. A deep line between his shining brown eyes told her he wasn't just saying these things to make her feel better.

A salty tear reached her upper lip. It tasted as bitter as she felt. 'Then why did you leave?'

Still holding her tightly, he stared at her, his lips slightly apart, as if there was so much he had to say but didn't know where to start. Then he squeezed his eyes shut and let his forehead fall forward onto hers. 'This isn't fair on you. It's time I told you the truth.'

'Told me the truth?' She pulled herself roughly out of his arms.

He stumbled forward slightly as she moved away, and snapped his eyes open.

'Isn't that what our trip down the Thames was all about? Laying some ghosts to rest was what you said.'

She wiggled her fingers to show inverted commas, and he cringed at having his own words used against him.

'Yes. I had intended to come clean with you that day, but when it came to it, there were some things that seemed better left unsaid.'

She pressed the side of her index finger onto her brow and span round, so she had her back to him. 'I don' believe this. No, wait. I completely believe this. I knew you were keeping something from me. But for God's sake, Toren!' She turned to face him again, her arms wide open, fingers splayed out. 'Don't you think I deserved to know the truth 10 years ago when you walked out on our marriage? Don't you think I deserved to know the truth two months ago when you strolled back into my office asking me for help? Why now? Why now after all these years?' Her hair, wet-through from the rain, lay limply against her black-streaked face. Her dress, once beautiful and floaty, now clung like a second skin to her shivering body.

'Come on, let's go home, you're freezing'. He stretched his arms towards her, but she backed away.

'No! Don't you dare. Don't you think you can do that to me. I don't care if I melt away down this bloody grate.' She pointed accusingly at the floor by his feet where running rainwater streamed into a drain. 'I'm not going anywhere until I get some answers.' She stepped towards him this time, and stopped only when she was millimetres away. She jutted her chin forward, and burned her eyes into his. 'And this time, you're not going to fob me off with some rubbish about you leaving because you couldn't bear to sit around and watch me hurt myself. Because we both know that's not true.'

He wiped a large raindrop off his nose before it had chance to splosh onto her face beneath him. 'That was the truth, Mimi. It was the truth.'

'Don't call me that,' she snapped.

He ran a hand through his hair, sending water trickling unpleasantly down the back of his neck. 'Okay, fine. But I'm telling you, everything I said to you that day was the absolute truth. There was just something I left out. Something important'

She swallowed, and blinked against the hammering rain several times, then folded her arms across her sodden chest.

'Well, you'd better spit it out then, because I've spent the last 10 years wondering what the hell I did so very wrong that even my husband couldn't stand being with me anymore.'

He reached out and touched her

elbow, expecting her to bolt away from him, but she didn't. 'It wasn't anything you did wrong.'

'Pah!' She let out a humourless laugh, and turned her face away from him. 'What? Don't tell me — it's not you, it's me? Please, save your breath if clichés are all you can manage.'

He pulled his hand away from her, and let it fall down his side, then tipped his head up to the sky. 'That's not what I was going to say.' He rubbed his eyes, then sunk his hands into his pockets. 'We can't talk here. Let's go somewhere.'

'I've told you — I'm going nowhere until I know what it is you've been holding back from me for the last 10 years.'

'See that light over there?'

She looked in the direction he was pointing, at the dimly lit window across the road.

'Yes?'

'It's a Nachtcafé.'

'A what?'

'A Nachtcafé. There are a few of them in the city. They're cafés that are open all night long. I've been there before. It has a quiet corner by the fire. We can dry off and talk in privacy.'

She seemed to consider it for a moment, then shrugged. 'Okay, but I'm serious, Toren. No more excuses.'

He nodded, and followed her as she made her way out of the alleyway several feet ahead of him. As they crossed the road she stumbled. He reached out to steady her, and she shrugged him off. 'I'm fine,' she muttered. He took his hands away, but made sure he stayed closer to her should she trip again.

★ ★ ★

The cup rocked slightly on the saucer as he set it on the table in front of her. The movement toppled the peak of the whipped cream, and sent a sliver of it running down the outside of the cup. She didn't acknowledge the drink, nor him as he slid it across the table to her.

He sat down on the chair beside her, and watched her expression as the crackling fire reflected against her skin. Her eyes were red-rimmed and blotchy, and her lips were swollen from crying. She looked worlds away from the elegant, polished woman who'd emerged from the limo, eyes glowing in anticipation of the ball. And it had all been just a few hours before. But to him she was every inch as beautiful now. How ugly must I seem to her? After all the hurt he'd caused her, and the half-truths he'd told her, it was time to put that right.

'I should have told you from the beginning.' His words were met with silence. The only sign she'd heard him was an ironic smile on her face as she continued to look forwards, at the flames. 'It's about Anya,' he continued.

She turned to look at him, her brow knitted. 'Your sister?'

He nodded.

'I don't understand.'

He took a sip of his treacle-black coffee. 'One thing I never told you, never told anyone actually, was that Anya was adopted.'

She pulled her legs up onto the chair and hugged her knees. 'Oh. Why not?'

'It was a family secret. Anya always knew, of course, and it never mattered when we were kids. Our parents treated us both the same, we argued like normal siblings.' He laughed gently as fond childhood memories flashed behind his eyes. 'It was only when Anya reached 16 that the problems started.'

'Problems?' Naomi reached forward and carefully picked up her cream-topped cup from the table. 'What happened?'

He sat forward toward the fire, and balanced his elbows on his knees. 'She'd never been interested in knowing her biological parents before then. But all of a sudden, a need to know where she came from seemed to take over her. She sat us all down one evening to tell us she was going to find her real mother.'

'That must have been tough for your parents. How did they react?'

Her words cut into his memory, reminding him she was there. That scene, around the kitchen table in their two-up two down family home, would be etched in his mind forever. As would the sound of his mother's sobs in the night, when she'd thought it safe to cry because her children were both asleep. He hadn't been. He'd been turning his sister's words over and over in his mind, hoping her plan didn't rip their beautiful family apart. But it had.

'Mum and Dad were torn up inside, I could see that. They thought they'd somehow failed because Anya was so desperate to find her real parents. They didn't let her know that, of course, and were fully supportive. They even helped her contact the authorities and trace her family.'

'She was lucky she had that support behind her. I can understand why she'd want to discover where she came from though. Your parents could see that, surely?'

He looked across at her. She had a cream moustache over her top lip, which usually he would find amusing, but he couldn't even muster a smile as the pain he'd felt over half his life ago was back with a vengeance.

'Yes. They could see her point of view. But they were still scared.'

'Scared of what?'

The fire suddenly seemed to grow fiercer. Intense heat crept up his neck, and he scratched at it coarsely. 'They thought she might meet her biological family, get to know them, and decide she belonged with them, rather than with us.'

Her hair was beginning to dry, and had crinkled around her face. He'd forgotten just how curly it used to be.

'And did she?'

'In the end, no. But in the beginning, it was a living hell for my parents, Mum especially.'

Her eyelids blinked over wide eyes, and she nodded to encourage him to go on.

'When we found them — her real family — she started to spend weekends with them. She even went on a month-long holiday with them. She had half siblings, and used to come home and talk about nothing else other than how they looked like her, and how she felt like she finally knew who she was. My parents did a great job at pretending they thought it was wonderful for her, but really it killed them to hear it.'

'Why? If it made her happy, then surely it was a good thing.'

'Because they'd brought her up. As far as they were concerned, she was their daughter. From her point of view, she'd gained a family. From theirs, they were in danger of losing a child.'

'I see,' she said. 'What happened in the end? You said things turned out okay.'

'Eventually, yes. But not after my

mum nearly had a breakdown because of it. Six months after meeting her real family for the first time, Anya decided to go and live with them permanently.'

Naomi's hand flew to her mouth. 'Oh, Toren. I had no idea. Your poor parents must have been beside themselves.'

'Yup. And it wasn't like they lived down the road. They were in Ireland. There was an ocean between us.'

'They wouldn't have been allowed to do that. Her real family I mean. The law doesn't allow parents to sweep in and claim their children back after giving them up for adoption.'

'It wasn't a matter of them taking her away. She was old enough to make her own decision. She chose to go.' He sniffed out a half-hearted laugh. 'When she told us she was going, I shouted and screamed at her, begged her to stay, tried to get her to see what it would do to Mum and Dad. She wouldn't listen. She was adamant she was going. Dad had to calm me down, saying we had to let her go, because we loved her so much.'

He felt Naomi's hand rest on his knee. He paused to savour the sensation of her against his skin before he continued. 'I didn't understand what he was talking about. I do now though, when I think about it with an adult head. Trying to convince her to stay would have been the wrong thing to do. If you love someone enough then you let them go.'

'I can't believe you've never told me this, Toren. When I met your family, everything seemed so perfect. Your parents and Anya couldn't have been more loving towards each other, and towards you.'

He nodded. 'Anya eventually came back, after a couple of months. She was a mess, crying, saying it had all gone wrong. She hadn't fitted in with her new family and felt like the odd one out. Her time away had given her a chance to think about how what she'd done had affected Mum and Dad. She couldn't have been sorrier, and begged us for forgiveness.'

'So, it all ended well?'

He looked up at her, and raised his eyebrows. 'Yeah, by chance, it did. It could have been a different story though. What if she had fitted in with her new family? We might never have seen her again.'

She gave his knee a squeeze. 'You're still annoyed at her, aren't you?'

He picked up his cup, and ran a finger up and down the side the side of it, pondering the question. 'Yes, I suppose I am. I understand why she felt the need to know where she came from, but she wasn't the one who had to pick up the pieces. I watched my mum almost kill herself with worry in the time Anya was gone. My dad cried, you know.'

The memory of finding his dad in the kitchen, wiping away tears he'd never seen him shed before, punctured his chest. 'That was a first for me, seeing my dad like that. And no, you're right, part of me will never forgive her for that.'

'You get on well now though, don't you?'

'Yes, Mum, Dad, Anya, they visit all the time. And they love Ali to bits too. But during those few months I saw things I'll never forget.'

She lowered her eyes, and chewed on her bottom lip. 'When you left, when we broke up, it was around the time we'd started talking about adopting, wasn't it?'

He pressed his lips together. He didn't have to answer her question to convey she was right.

'That day on the boat . . . when I said to you I left because I couldn't bear to watch you get hurt, I meant it. Going through the IVF, and all the pain it caused you, was bad enough, but then you started to talk about adoption it brought it all back. I'd already seen my mother go through hell because her daughter decided to find her real family. There was no way on earth I was

254

going to watch the love of my life endure that same torment.'

'Oh, Toren. Why didn't you tell me? We didn't have to adopt. If we couldn't have children, then so be it. Our marriage didn't have to end because of it.'

'I'm so sorry.' He clutched her hand, and weaved his fingers through hers. 'I didn't think the experience had affected me so much. I couldn't put it into words back then, I was confused. I thought if I cited that as the reason I didn't want to adopt, you'd think me selfish, and crazy. And you'd be right. It was a selfish and crazy reason not to take on a child that needs a home. I thought if I left, then at least you could go on to adopt with another man. Someone who didn't carry that kind of baggage around with him. Under the circumstances, leaving seemed to be the kindest option.'

She slipped her hand away from under his, and sat back in her chair, leant her head on the backrest and closed her eyes. 'Thank you for being so honest. The tragedy is, though, it's too late to change anything now.' Her voice was calm and even, and laced with such deep regret it cut deep into him and smothered his own heart in a thick, black sadness.

He watched the jewels on her dress glint in the firelight. He'd broken the family secret, laid his soul on the line, told her everything, and yet she was right. None of it mattered now.

13

'Naomi's taking me out? For the whole day?' Ali's eyes sparkled as she confirmed the news Toren gave her.

'That's right,' he said, smiling at his daughter's enthusiasm. 'So, you'd better hurry up and get ready. She'll be here in an hour.'

'In one hour? Why didn't you tell me earlier, Dad? I've got so much to do to get ready.'

He laughed. 'All you've got to do is clean your teeth, comb your hair and get dressed. That should take about 10 minutes. The chocolate croissants will be out of the oven in a matter of seconds, so that's breakfast taken care of.'

'Dad, you have no idea what us girls need to do to get ready.' Ali rolled her eyes to add emphasis to her dramatic declaration.

'No, you're probably right there,' he admitted, and pulled open the oven door.

'How could you think I'd have time for breakfast when I only have one hour to get ready?'

A waft of freshly-baked pastry filled the kitchen, and made his mouth water. Ali obviously caught it too, for by the time he'd taken the tray out of the oven, she was already sat at the table.

'Oh,' he said, feigning surprise. 'I thought there was no time to eat.'

'Well, breakfast is the most important meal of the day,' she answered, pouring herself a glass of orange juice from the carton.

'I see.' He set a plate of steaming croissants in the centre of the table.

'Thanks, Dad.' Ali took one, pulled off a loose strand of pastry, and popped it into her mouth.

'Where's Naomi taking me?' she asked between bites.

'Down to the coast, I think.'

'The seaside? How cool! Will we be

able to go swimming in the sea?'

'I doubt it, sweetheart. Not unless you want to turn into an ice cube. It is the end of October, and this is Brighton we're talking about, not Barbados.'

'Oh.' Her face fell momentarily before quickly lighting up again. 'Maybe we'll go shopping then, and have ice cream, or rock even!'

'Maybe. Whatever Naomi's got planned, I'm sure you'll have a great day.'

'Definitely.' Ali nodded in agreement. She fell silent and chewed quickly, clearly eager to get on with whatever was involved in her getting ready process. Having wolfed down two croissants, she excused herself from the table and dashed off upstairs, leaving Toren to contemplate what his daughter's day would be like.

Naomi had explained — over email, as they hadn't seen each other or spoken since their return from Vienna — that the final part of her due diligence involved spending time with

259

Ali to see if she could illicit vital information regarding his suitability as a father.

He'd read those words over and over, and every time they cut deeper. His suitability as a father, for God's sake. He'd brought Ali up since she was a tiny baby. He nursed her when she was ill, cheered on her first steps, and dried her tears when her mother failed to show up for the meetings he arranged. Was she suggesting he was in some way an unsuitable parent?

Naomi must have picked up on his annoyance in his curt response, as she replied with a more sensitive explanation as to why it could help.

If there's any nugget of information she could pick up through talking to Ali, then it could make all the difference to the outcome.

He'd do anything — anything at all — to keep Ali, and so he agreed.

If nothing else, Naomi had written, she'll have a great day out. That he didn't doubt. He knew how much his daughter adored Naomi, and if he were honest with himself, he suspected the feeling was mutual — not that Naomi would be so unprofessional to admit it.

By the time the doorbell rang indicating Naomi's arrival, Ali was already waiting by the door.

'Ooh, she's here!' she squealed, and tugged at the door handle.

'Here, let me help,' laughed Toren, and opened the door. Naomi was dressed casually in jeans, cowboy boots and a striped knitted jumper under a mac. The look suited her.

'Hi,' was all he could manage. He'd said so much in Vienna — too much. He'd opened his very soul up to her, and now, in the broad light of day, he was embarrassed at having done so.

'Hi,' she said back. He thought he detected a flicker of uncharacteristic nervousness in her eyes. She's probably embarrassed for me.

'Hello,' piped up Ali, gloriously unaware of the awkwardness between the adults. She peered around Naomi, her forehead knitting into a frown. 'Where's your car?'

Naomi broke into a smile. 'I thought we'd get the train. Is that okay with you?' She directed the question at him, although Ali answered before he had a chance.

'The train?' She jumped up and down, the rucksack on her back jiggling precariously. 'Yes, yes, yes, yes yes, yes. I haven't been on a train for years!'

He laughed. 'Well, that's a slight exaggeration, but I guess it has been quite a while.'

'Can I, Daddy? Can I, can I? Pleeeease can I?'

'Yes, of course. Just remember your manners, and Naomi's in charge today, so follow her rules.'

'Thanks Dad, you're the best dad in the world ever!' She squeezed him tightly round the waist.

'I know. 'Cos I'm the only one you got!' They said the last sentence in unison, as they always did. It was a saying of theirs, that usually rolled off the tongue without second thought. But today he realised it may not actually be true. The court case was less than a week away. This time next week if things didn't go his way, Ali could be living with a different dad.

The thought caught in his chest, and instantly dried out his throat. He hugged his daughter back, and forced out a cough, but his words still came out coarse. 'Have a wonderful day, pumpkin.'

'Come on, Ali.' Naomi held her hand out for Ali to take. 'Better get going or we'll miss the train.'

She knew what was going through my head. Knew I almost lost it just then. He was grateful to Naomi for hurrying up the farewell to avoid him losing composure in front of his little girl. He needed to hold himself together, if not for him, then at least for her.

* * *

Naomi pulled at the lid of her polystyrene carton. It opened with a squeak, and a whiff of salt and vinegar permeated her nostrils. 'Do you come to the seaside much with your dad?' she asked, then crunched her teeth through the crispy batter to the hot fish inside.

Ali shook her head, and popped a chip into her mouth. 'Dad brought me here once I think, when I was little, but we spend most Christmas holidays in our chalet in France, and at Easter we usually go to our apartment in New York, or our villa in the Caribbean. I'd rather come here, though.'

Naomi smiled. Ali was a very grounded little girl, which was testament to Toren's parenting. It would be so easy for her to be a spoilt madam considering how privileged she was.

'You'd rather come to Brighton than all those amazing places your dad takes you?'

Ali shrugged and shifted her bottom on the pebbles to get comfortable. 'Maybe. I like eating fish and chips on the beach fresh out of the box. And I like the funny little shops in Brighton, and coming here on the train. It's fun.'

'Not so great in winter though, hey?'

Ali threw a chip for a seagull to feast on. 'Nah, and I think I'd miss skiing if we didn't go to France.'

'Did your dad teach you to ski?'

Ali battled to cut her fish with the side of her miniature wooden fork. 'Yep. And snowboard. And swim. And ride a bike. Daddy taught me everything, 'cos my mum didn't want me.'

Naomi felt as though that wooden fork had pierced her heart when Ali said those words. 'It might not have been that simple, Ali. Your mum was very young when she had you, and perhaps not ready to look after a child.'

'It's okay,' she said, matter-of-factly, and looked directly at Naomi with big tearless eyes. 'I don't feel sad about it anymore.'

'Anymore?'

Ali nodded again. 'I used to cry a lot, when I was little, 'cos she wouldn't turn up when Dad arranged for us to meet. But now, I'm glad it's just me and Dad. I get to keep him all to myself!' She broke into a toothy grin, and Naomi's heart melted more than she cared to admit to herself. 'Anyway,' Ali continued. 'Dad does all the dad stuff and all the mum stuff put together, so it's like having both parents.'

Naomi looked down towards the beach, and saw a young mother, trousers rolled up to her knees, holding hands with a toddler, who was jumping excitedly over the small waves as they crashed on the shoreline. What must it feel like to do that; to be there when your own little person discovered a new experience? You'll never know. The fork in her heart twisted, and she forced herself to focus.

'What kind of mum stuff does your dad do?' she asked Ali, through a scratchy throat.

Having finished her lunch, Ali picked up a smooth, round pebble and inspected it. 'Y'know, bakes cakes, takes me shopping, lets me put make-up on him, that kinda stuff.'

Naomi laughed, trying to imagine the debonair, business-like Toren with a face plastered in lipstick and eyeshadow.

'I thought Pippa did all that.'

'Oh yeah, she does sometimes. But Dad often gives her the day off, and does it with me instead.' Then she turned to Naomi and whispered conspiratorially, as if the seagulls might be spies interested in their conversation. 'I think he likes to spend time with me.' Ali rolled her eyes at this, but Naomi could tell by her smile that the little girl enjoyed spending time with her father just as much as he did with her.

Without thinking, she reached out and squeezed Ali's hand. 'You're very lucky,' she whispered back. Emotion swelled in her chest, and her eyes began to sting. Ali's smile faded, and she cocked her head to the side. 'Does your daddy not like spending time with you?'

She exhaled slowly to stop herself

losing her composure at the little girl's concern, and innocent words. 'Oh yes. I mean, he did. He died though, unfortunately.' She coughed back a sob, which threatened to rise.

'That's sad,' said Ali, showing no trace of awkwardness like an adult might under the same circumstances. 'I don't want my dad to ever die.'

'You don't have to worry about that, pumpkin.' She realised she'd adopted the pet name that Toren gave Ali, and mentally chastised herself for her uncharacteristic lack of professionalism. 'I'm sure your dad will live long enough to drive you mad when you're all grown up yourself.' She laughed, but Ali didn't join in. Her eyebrows hooded her pretty blue eyes, creating a forlorn expression.

'What if he's not my dad by the time I get older.'

'What do you mean, Ali?'

The little girl hugged her knees and dug her heels into the pebbles. 'I know I'm only nine, but I'm not a baby. I know what's happening — that my mum wants me to go live with her. Will I see Daddy again?' She looked up at Naomi, her eyes squinting against the golden autumnal sun.

This is not how she envisaged the conversation going. She searched her brain for the best answer she could think of. Ali looked so innocent, so wounded. Her angelic face looked up at Naomi, and hope shone in her eyes — a hope that Naomi could give her some kind of reassurance that she could stay with her father.

Still at a loss for words, she stroked a hair away from Ali's face, and placed an arm around her tiny shoulders. 'I can't answer that, sweetheart, but what I can say is that your dad loves you very, very much, and always will.'

'And making sure he gets to keep me is your job, right?'

Naomi pressed her lips together in a pathetic attempt at a reassuring smile, and gave a slight nod. What do I say to that?

Ali's shoulders dropped with relief,

and she grinned again.

She's counting on me. She trusts me. Suddenly, the meal she'd so enthusiastically devoured felt heavy and greasy in her stomach, leaving her feeling slightly sick. I have to win this case, she thought. For Toren, for his little girl, and — stark realisation hit her square in the gut — for herself. It was too late to back off. The fight was personal.

'He likes you, you know?'

'What?' She snapped out of her thoughts, and realised what Ali had said.

'Dad. He likes you.'

'Well, I like him too. We work well together.'

'No. I mean he really likes you. He wants you to be his girlfriend.'

'Oh, I'm sure that's not true.' She laughed in a bid to stifle the butterflies going crazy in her stomach.

'It is true. He goes all strange when he's on the phone to you, or if he knows you're coming around.'

'What do you mean, strange?' she

asked, not sure she wanted to hear the answer.

'You know, all weird. His eyes go funny, like he's nervous or something. And Dad never gets nervous.'

'I see. Maybe he needs glasses.'

Ali broke into a fit of giggles. 'He wears contact lenses, silly!'

Does he? He never did when we were . . .

'And anyway, it was you in the photo.' Ali raised an eyebrow.

'What photo?'

'Remember what I said that when I first met you, when Dad took you on the boat that time? I asked Dad if it was you in his photograph.'

Naomi nodded.

'And Dad pretended he didn't know what I was talking about? Well, I sneaked into his study, and looked in his top drawer. It was right there. He'd tried to hide it under a load of papers, but I still found it. You looked different in the picture, but it was definitely you.'

'I'm sure your dad has lots of old photos around.'

'Nope. He has lots of me, and a couple of old black and white ones of people I don't know, but no others. Only the one of you.'

'Oh.' It was a stupid thing to say, but she was at a loss for words. So Toren had wanted to remember her, after all these years. What the hell did that mean?

'I think you like him too. Do you wish he was your boyfriend?' She leaned in towards Ali, and whispered again. 'I think secretly you do.'

She thought back to the night in Vienna when, dripping wet from the downpour, Toren had held her, and opened his heart to her. She'd never felt so close to him, even in the days when they'd been madly in love, before it all went wrong. And she questioned, really questioned, whether Ali was the only one out of the three of them who could see the truth. She couldn't possibly admit to a nine-year-old she was in love with her father — not when she wasn't ready to admit it to herself. But nor could she lie to her.

'Now you're being the silly one!' She gave Ali a playful nudge on the arm, and returned her grin. 'Come on, you. This greedy seagull you've been feeding will be calling his friends anytime soon, and we'll be surrounded by the pesky things.' She pulled Ali up by her hand, and together they made their way off the pebbles toward the promenade.

14

Toren massaged his temples to try and ease the tension in his skull, but it had little effect. The court case was two days away. He'd barely slept all week. The night terrors had made sure of that. After what felt like minutes of finally dropping off he'd wake up drenched in sweat. In his recurrent nightmare, Ali was being dragged away by a faceless creature, screaming and shouting for him. He longed to run to her, to save her, but shackles held him tightly, so he couldn't move. He couldn't get to his little girl when she needed him most.

'Tor.' A brunette head popped round the side of the door. 'Would you mind finishing off Ali's bonfire guy with her? This horrible cold's got the better of me. I'm going to have to go for a lie down, I'm afraid, before I fall down.'

'Sure, Pip,' he said. 'No problem. I'll be there in just a second, you get yourself some rest.'

'Thanks. We've been working on the thing for two hours already, but she's determined to get him just right. There's a best guy competition at the fireworks event tonight, and you know how competitive your daughter is.'

He nodded without fully taking in exactly what his nanny was saying.

'Are you okay, Tor?'

Pippa's words grabbed his attention, and he turned to face her.

'Okay? Yes, yes, I'm fine thanks. You take yourself to bed, Pippa. Concentrate on getting well. Would you like me to make you a hot lemon?'

'Erm, I got one already.' She pointed to the huge mug she was clearly holding in front of her.

'Oh right, I see.'

She paused and frowned. 'Are you sure you're okay?'

He was touched at her concern, but wasn't in the mood to start opening up about his feelings as men were expected to do these days. The only thing that's going to help me right now is to be proactive, and do whatever I can to keep my daughter.

He nodded, and was relieved when she finally left. Good old Pippa. She was so reliable, and trustworthy. And Ali loved her.

For the first time ever, it occurred to him how she would be affected if he did lose Ali. He could keep her on as housekeeper of course, but she too would have to say goodbye to the little girl she'd looked after for the past two years. I'm so wrapped up in myself I haven't even spared a thought to how Pippa's coping with all this. Shame washed over him, like he'd just swallowed a bad pill.

'Da-ad. Can you help me with this guy please? I wanna win this competition.'

At the sound of Ali calling from the kitchen, he smiled in spite of himself.

She was competitive, all right, just as

he was. She was his daughter through and through, biologically or not. Renewed strength filled his veins. He wasn't just fighting for himself and Pippa, and what they faced losing. He was fighting for Ali too.

'Coming, pumpkin,' he said, with a new sense of vigour. 'Let's win this thing!'

* * *

Toren tried in vain to remove the glue and felt from his fingers as his phone rang, insistently.

Ali glared at him with a look that said, 'Don't get distracted, Dad, we haven't finished yet.' They'd been working on the model for over an hour, and he'd spent at least half of that trying to convince his daughter that their model replica of Guy Fawkes was definitely a contender for first prize.

She was having none of it, though, the perfectionist that she was, and was still determinedly cutting out minute bits of fabric for him to stick on to decorate the guy's colourful waistcoat.

Having finally managed to extricate enough gunk from his fingers to pick up the handset, he touched the screen to accept the call.

'Toren, it's me, Naomi.'

She didn't need to confirm her identity. He'd know her velvety smooth voice anywhere. 'Hi. Everything all right? Is the case still on for Monday?'

'Yes, that's all still going ahead.'

His heart sank. For a millisecond he'd allowed himself to hope it might have been called off; that Michelle had done something good for once in her life, by realising her daughter was settled with him, and had called off the case. His heart sank down to his size 11s when Naomi confirmed that had not happened.

'Can I pop over for an hour this evening? I just want to make sure we're both fully clear on Monday's proceedings. I know we met last week to go through them, but it would be good for both of us to get them fresh in our mind seeing as the hearing is only two days away.'

As if he needed reminding. He'd thought about nothing else for weeks.

'Tonight? Yes, sure. Whatever we need to do.'

Ali shook her head vehemently and mouthed to him fireworks.

'Oh, sorry, I forgot, although I don't know how I could,' he said, surveying the mess of craft materials on the table in front of him. 'Ali and I are going to the fireworks event at her school tonight. Can we make it tomorrow?'

Naomi was saying something down the line to him, but he couldn't make out what it was as Ali waved her arms around, desperate to get his attention.

'Is it Naomi, Dad?' she asked. 'Is it Naomi? Is it?'

'Pumpkin, please, I'm on the phone.'

'Are you on the phone to Naomi?'

He gave up trying to hear what Naomi was saying. 'For goodness sake, yes, I am.'

'Ask her to come to fireworks night. Ask her, Dad, ask her, please.'

'I take it you heard that invitation,' he said into the handset. 'Would you like to come to fireworks with us tonight? We'll be home by eight. Perhaps we can talk then.'

Silence on the other end of the line.

'Naomi? Are you still there?'

'Yes. I'm still here. Okay. Why not? I haven't been to fireworks since — well, I can't even remember when. What time shall I come by?'

★ ★ ★

Toren stood in the seemingly never-ending hotdog queue with a host of other parents. Winter had arrived in all its glory tonight, and the air was cold, crisp and clear. Remember, remember, the fifth of November. The rhyme went around and round in his head. How on earth could he forget? In two days' time, he'd learn his fate — and that of his daughter.

He looked over at where she stood, with the one woman who could save them. Naomi. The sight of their silhouettes, stark and black against the orange blaze of the bonfire, warmed the inside of his chest. Ali's small, mittened hand was held by Naomi, who was pointing out the helpers setting up the famous Catherine Wheel firework.

In another life, they could be his family. He'd collect their hotdogs and hot chocolates, and walk over, take them both in his arms, and they'd watch the show, oohing and aahing together with the rest of the crowd. Like the normal families surrounding them. They didn't know how lucky they were.

The heat around his heart dissipated, leaving him frozen on the inside and out. They weren't a normal family. Naomi wasn't even part of his family. That was his doing. And however much he wished things were different . . .

A thought occurred to him. A thought so positive it lifted his spirits higher than any firework. He would tell her tonight. He would tell her how he felt; that he wanted her back, and had never, ever stopped loving her. It had always been her. Always Naomi. Why not? And why hadn't he done it already? At this point he had nothing to lose.

He was so energised at the prospect, he almost floated over to them, not even caring the flimsy cardboard cups were burning his fingers. 'There you go, madam. It's hot, be careful.' He handed Ali a cup overflowing with whipped cream and marshmallows. 'And a mulled wine for you.'

'Thanks.' Naomi took her drink, and their eyes locked.

How will she react when I tell her? A cloud of doubt darkened his resolve. It was so close to the court hearing. Would it ruin everything? He couldn't possibly do it if it meant sabotaging his chances of losing the case and keeping Ali. But nor could he deny his love for Naomi. It was consuming his every moment, and this might be his last chance to tell her how he felt, for after the court hearing, she'd be out of his life for good. On the other hand, his daughter meant the world to him, and he would gladly forsake his own happiness to ensure hers. The impossible dilemma melted into a pool of depression at the pit of his stomach. What a bloody awful mess he'd created.

A whizz followed by a loud bang wrenched him out of his thoughts.

'Look, Daddy, the fireworks have started. Can I go on your shoulders?'

'You're a bit big for that now, aren't you, pumpkin?'

Naomi and Ali simultaneously shot him a look that would have scared the hardest criminal.

'Okay, okay, I can see I'm outnumbered.' He laughed, and held up his hands in surrender. Ali lifted up her arms to him, just as she had as a toddler, and he swooped her up, and settled her on his shoulders. He squeezed his eyes shut, and savoured the warmth of her little arms clasping his neck. Normally he'd look up at her, and with a mock strangled voice, tell her to ease up, but tonight he didn't want her to ever let go. A tear slid down his cheek, and dried in a cold pool by the corner of his mouth.

A glove-padded hand rested on his lower back. He turned his head to the side and saw Naomi giving him a watery smile. There she goes again, knowing exactly what I'm thinking. Only she had ever possessed the ability to do that. And at that moment, he made his decision.

15

'I can't believe after all that work, we forgot to take the guy tonight. Now we'll never know if we'd have won the competition.'

'I didn't forget, Daddy,' called Ali as she skipped along the pavement in between him and Ali on the way back from the fireworks. 'All the guys are put on top of the bonfire. I didn't want mine to be burned to a crisp!'

Toren laughed, and dug his key out of his coat pocket. A few more steps and they'd be at their front door. 'I suppose it would have been a waste. All those hours of work go up in smoke.'

'That's not the reason.' Ali looked up at him as he turned the key in the lock. 'If I don't get to stay living with you, then I'll keep the guy forever, as a reminder of you. It will be the last thing we made together.'

He went to speak, but his words disappeared into the cold night air, along with his visible breath.

'Come on, then,' Naomi said. 'Let's get inside, away from the cold. I know a little girl who is very, very tired.'

She took the key from his fumbling fingers, and with one turn unlocked the door. He was vaguely aware of Ali denying her tiredness, but her earlier words had stung too much for him to take in what was going on. That's why she'd taken so much care over making the guy; why she'd insisted they'd spent hours creating it together. Because she knew it could be the last time. Darn. It's happening. This is real.

His next 20 minutes were trance-like. He sat on the sofa in front of the fire. A brandy had somehow been put in his hand, but he hadn't poured it himself. Ali, in her pyjamas, kissed him on the cheek and said goodnight. He responded, but could barely hear his own words. Naomi mentioned something about tucking her in. He nodded, as if a puppeteer was in charge of his head movements.

'Toren. Toren. Are you ready?' Naomi's voice, somewhere in the distance.

'Ready?'

'To go through the last-minute details. Before the hearing.' She wasn't in the distance — she was right there, on the sofa next to him.

'The hearing?'

'Yes. The hearing on Monday. Toren, are you all right?'

He drained his glass. The alcohol stung his throat, but strangely enough, brought lucidity back into his head. 'Be honest with me, Naomi. Do we stand a chance?'

She pressed her lips together, and dropped her gaze. 'Yes. We stand a chance. A good chance, but it's by no means a done deal. I've been doing some digging, and the opposition has filed a strong case. We've got our work cut out, no doubt about it.'

'Thank you.' He leaned forward and placed his empty glass on the coffee table. 'For being frank with me. I understand there's a lot of pressure on you right now, and you've been incredible, Naomi, throughout this whole process.'

'There's no point in not being honest,' she said, batting away the compliment.

'I couldn't agree more. Which is why you deserve some honesty from me in return.'

She held up her hands, and shook her head. 'Please, Toren. I don't think I can cope with any more revelations.' She followed her words with a sardonic laugh. 'As if turning up unannounced in my office weren't enough to deal with, you then tell me you left me because you couldn't bear to watch me getting hurt, then you drop the bombshell about not wanting to adopt because of what happened with your sister. Please don't tell me there's more. Not at this stage in the game when we need to focus on the hearing.'

'Naomi, I am hopelessly, painfully

and desperately in love with you. I thought if we spent enough time apart I'd learn to live without you — forget you even — but I was an idiot for thinking that. Working with you, being with you over these last few months has made me admit to myself what I always knew deep down — that there is no-one for me but you.'

He braced himself for a torrent of backlash, God knows he deserved it, or for her to storm out. But she said nothing; did nothing. Just silence. Seconds ticked by, and his mind raced, as he tried to fathom why she wasn't protesting. Then it dawned. He snapped his head up to meet her eyes. 'You feel the same, don't you?'

She looked away, and shook her head. But it was more in objection than in denial.

'You do, don't you? Naomi . . . '

'Toren, please, don't.'

He held her hand, and entwined his fingers through hers. 'You do, don't you?'

Their bodies were so close. Their foreheads touched. He lowered his eyes, and saw her chin wobble.

'Yes.' The word escaped her mouth in a whimper, but he was in no doubt he'd heard it.

'Naomi . . . ' Barely had he spoken her name when their mouths locked together in a kiss. The fireworks they'd watched an hour ago now exploded in his brain. Bright colours, bangs, fizzes, pure exhilaration filled his head. The intimacy between them grew. Her flesh filled his hands. His own skin tingled beneath her touch. The soft curves of her body pressed against his firmness. Their lips barely parted from one another's. He lowered his eyelids, but never closed them. He wanted constant reassurance this was real.

He didn't recall them undressing each other, but it must have happened somehow in their tangle of limbs, because her skin was on his. And without speaking, without thinking, without trying, they were united. It wasn't like it had been before. They were different people now — harder, damaged, but as a result their love-making was even more tender. He was floating again. Like he had the night they'd danced together. Soaring, higher and higher together, until, in perfect harmony, they reached the ultimate precipice.

★ ★ ★

The rattle of a key in a lock stirred Naomi from her sleep. It took her a few seconds to remember where she was, who she was with, and what state of undress she was in, but not as many as it took Pippa to walk through the door of the living room.

'Hi guys, did you miss me? Oh, my goodness. Sorry! There I go bursting in on you two again. I seem to be making a habit out of it.'

She clearly hadn't banked on finding her employer huddled on the sofa with his lawyer, both of them naked apart from a furniture throw.

'Pippa, hi.'

How could he sound so casual? Toren had never been one for caring what other people thought, but this was an extreme situation to be caught.

'Erm, I know it's Sunday, but do you realise what time it is? I'm surprised Ali isn't up yet.' Her eyes widened. 'She isn't, is she?'

Naomi lowered her head into the blanket to avoid Pippa from seeing her burning cheeks. Shame overcame her. Ali could have caught us!

Toren laughed, obviously more relaxed than she felt. 'No. She had a late night. I don't expect she'll be down for a while.'

'Right.' Pippa bit her bottom lip. 'Well, just to be sure, I'll go up and if she is awake I'll keep her talking in her room for a while to give you two time to — you know.'

'Great, thanks Pip,' he said.

'Oh. My. Goodness.' Naomi tipped her head up to look at him. 'How could we be so careless?' she said, once Pippa had clicked the door shut.

He tightened his arms around her waist, and pulled her up until their faces met. 'Don't worry.' He placed a gentle kiss on her lips. 'I know my little girl. She likes her bed too much. She won't surface for at least another hour. Do you think I'd let her find us like this?'

'I don't know.' She pulled away from his kisses. 'Would you?'

He propped himself up his arm. 'No, but if she did would it be such a problem?'

'Well, yes, of course it would. Don't you think letting your daughter find you scantily clad with your lawyer is somewhat inappropriate?'

He raised his eyebrows, and tipped the corners of his mouth down, as if contemplating. 'I think we firmly established last night that you love me. And I most definitely love you, so what's bad about two people in love cuddling on the sofa? Anyway, Ali would be delighted to find her match-making efforts have finally paid off!'

She let out a breathy laugh. 'What were we thinking, Toren?'

He planted another kiss on her mouth. 'I don't know about you, but last night I didn't have to do much thinking. Everything felt so natural. Perfect, in fact.'

There was no point denying he was right, so she nodded. 'But what now?'

'Now,' he tucked a rogue strand of hair behind her ear, 'we win this case. We keep Ali.'

We. How wonderful that sounded.

'And then?'

His gaze was intent, his smile faded. 'Then, we start living together as a family. If that's what you want, of course. It's long overdue.'

Her words caught in her throat, and her heart swelled. It was all she could do to nod her agreement.

'Better get moving then. Ali might be a sleepy-head, but if there's one thing more powerful than her need to sleep, it's her appetite. She'll be down here demanding breakfast in no time.'

★   ★   ★

'Ready?'

Toren's eyes, as dark as they had been at their first meeting, stared unblinkingly back at her. The rain lashed down on the grim London Monday. They were both dressed professionally in black, and Naomi couldn't help thinking they looked more appropriate for a funeral than a courtroom.

He nodded, and she noticed his Adam's apple bob inside his pale throat. He seemed to have lost weight overnight, and his shirt hung loose on his body. The sight of him, so drawn and sallow, made her heart ache.

A very different man from the one she'd said goodbye to yesterday now stood beside her at the foot of the courtroom's stone steps. After their night together, a renewed energy had seemed to overtake him. He was youthful, spirited, happy even. Their lovemaking had changed him. It had changed both of them if the truth be known. Never before had she prepared to stand before a judge, and fight for a cause so personal to her.

Normally, Toren was the kind of man who led the way, but this time he showed no willingness to budge from the spot on which he was rooted.

'Come on.' Her defiant tone masked her own uncharacteristic nerves. 'We've got this.' She longed to take him by the hand, but was aware that being seen to have any sort of relationship with her client could be considered gross misconduct if the opposition got a whiff of it. The only thing she could do under the circumstances was to nudge him gently on the arm. It had the desired effect, spurring him into motion. She took the steps to the courtroom entrance two at a time, and led her ex-husband, and forever love, through the intimidating, heavy door. To find out the fate of their family.

★   ★   ★

Naomi stepped inside Toren's living room. The sofa on which they'd made love stood right in front of her. On it sat Ali's beaming guy. The one she and Toren had spent hours making. The one Ali had deliberately avoided taking to the bonfire, because she wanted something to remember her father by. In case the unthinkable should happen. She squeezed her eyes closed to shut out the guy with his manic grin. 'I'm so, so, sorry, Toren.'

He didn't speak, just wrapped his arms around her from behind, and nestled his head onto her shoulder. 'Don't apologise. It's not your fault.'

'Yes, it is. I let you down. I let all of us down.'

He came around to face her, and his red-rimmed eyes burned into hers. 'I don't ever want to hear you say that again, do you understand? You did everything you could. You left no stone unturned. Michelle's case was so strong, no-one could have done better than you, Naomi, no-one.'

She thudded her head against his chest. 'It doesn't matter, though does it?' Her words were absorbed into his shirt. 'It doesn't matter how much you loved her, how much I loved her, how hard we both worked to keep her. The result is still the same. She's gone. We lost her'

She wept into the white cotton of his expensive shirt, blackening it with smudges of mascara.

'Stay with me, Naomi,' he whispered, resting his chin on the top of her head.

She looked up at him, her vision blurred with tears. 'How can you say that? Now, after everything? How can you still want me after I lost your little girl?'

'Because I love you. Losing Ali is bad enough. I can't lose you too.'

She couldn't stop shaking her head. 'No, no, no, no. I can't stay, I can't. Not now. Not now Ali's gone.'

He cupped her face in his hands.

'The way I feel about you hasn't changed, Naomi. I said it the other day, and I'll say it again. I'll say it every day until the day I die. I love you. We'll get Ali back. We can appeal, right?'

'Appeal?' Funny, the thought had never occurred to her, even though it's the first thing she would normally say to the few clients whose cases she lost. Appeal, appeal, don't give up. Never give up. This time, however, her energy levels were completely depleted. 'Yes, you can appeal. But not with me. Find yourself a different lawyer — a better one. I'll put you in touch with the best.'

'You are the best. It has to be you.'

'That's what you said before. You were wrong then, and you're wrong now.'

'No, Naomi. I need you. In more ways than one.'

He tried to keep her face in his palms, but she pulled away from his grasp. 'No, Toren, you're wrong. I have to go.' She headed for the door, and fumbled with the latch, desperate to get out, to get some air, to get away from his cries begging her to stay.

16

Nine months later. Naomi frowned at her car's navigation system. Stupid thing. The journey had been a nightmare from the moment she'd got out of London's congestion zone. There were roadworks everywhere, an accident had held her up for half an hour, and now it seemed that Mr Forester — the new client she'd been assigned — lived in the middle of nowhere.

Richard Chailey had warned her about this when she gave him her ultimatum nine months ago — let her transfer to property law, or she'd hand in her resignation.

To say her boss hadn't taken kindly to her request was an understatement, but as hard-nosed as Chailey was, he could see she was serious. Losing Toren's case — and losing Ali — had damaged her too deeply. With her confidence in shatters, and the huge burden of guilt, which hung like weights round her neck every single day, there was no way she could return to family law.

Property law in her practice may not be as lucrative or fast-paced as family law, but at least bricks and mortar didn't have hearts she could break. It was better that way, she told herself, even if it did mean having to meander her Mercedes down narrow English lanes to visit wealthy country-dwelling clients.

Dee thought she'd lost her mind. After everything she'd worked for she was giving it all up? Just because of one lousy man? Her friend had tried talking her round, and had even suggested she go back to Torrid since she'd been so unhappy without him. But that was one thing she could never do. The gaping hole Ali left would be a constant reminder of her failure.

'Oh, my apologies, Sat Nav,' she said to the electronic console in the centre of her car. 'You were right, after all. Five-hundred yards on the left. Ta-dah, and here we are.'

She swung her car on to the gravelled drive, silenced the ignition, and climbed out of the driver's seat. She paused for a moment, taking in the beautiful house before her, not quite believing what she was seeing. She took off her sunglasses, and squinted against the bright August sunshine.

Under the pale blue sky, and surrounded by its lush green garden, Mr Forester's home was the quintessential English country mansion. It was large, but not intimidatingly so. A picture-postcard thatched roof graced the top of the beautiful old building like a perfect gingerbread cottage. It was the kind of house she'd dreamed of owning — the kind of house she and Toren had talked about one day bringing their children up in. She shook the memory out of her head. 'Onwards and upwards, Naomi, onwards and upwards.'

The welcoming red front door

seemed to call her. She made her way over to it, her stiletto heels wobbling slightly as she negotiated the terrain. 'Made more for people with walking boots and Labradors than pencil skirts and high heels,' she said to herself, wondering when, after months of working in the property side of the firm, she would learn than client visits to the country required a very different work wardrobe to that she'd been used to.

A smiling middle-aged woman opened the door dressed in jeans and a casual pullover. 'Ah, you must be the lawyer, Ms Graham. We've been expecting you.'

'That's right.' Naomi held out hand, and the woman shook it. 'And you must be Mrs Forester?'

'Yes, my dear, I am.' Her hand was dainty and soft inside Naomi's. 'Please, do come in.'

She walked through the door into a country-styled kitchen complete with white Aga and stable door, which she presumed must lead to the rest of the house. The airy kitchen offered a wonderful sanctuary from the stifling heat outside. Out of courtesy she slipped off her shoes, and felt the refreshing coolness from the flagstone floor soar all the way up her calves.

'Now, my dear,' Mrs Forester clasped her hands together, and beamed. 'Can I get you a nice cold drink, while I fetch the man of the house?'

She smiled back, and it struck her how genteel and old-fashioned it was that Mrs Forester referred to her husband as the man of the house. 'That would be lovely, thank you.'

'Certainly, my love. How about you make yourself comfortable in the drawing room while I let him know you're here?' She gestured toward an archway, through which Naomi could just about make out the corner of a huge brown leather sofa.

The woman walked spryly away, and Naomi did as she'd suggested, making her way through the arch to the drawing room. The sight of the room in all its glory stopped her in her tracks. Like the kitchen it was traditionally but tastefully decorated with a dark wooden floor, huge cream rug, and expensive but lived-in furniture. An original inglenook fireplace stood at centre stage. Above the fireplace was an exquisitely-painted portrait of a young girl. She squinted at the painting. It couldn't be, could it?

'Ms Graham, is homemade lemonade okay for you?'

She spun around. Mrs Forester was standing behind her, holding out a glass for her to take.

'Y-yes, thank you.' She took the glass with a shaking hand.

'Are you all right, my dear?'

'No. I mean, yes. I'm fine, thank you. It's just that girl.'

Mrs Forester wrinkled her forehead. 'The girl?'

'The girl in the picture.' She turned her head to indicate the portrait above the fireplace. 'I thought . . . I thought for a moment she was someone I knew, but she can't possibly be.'

Mrs Forester broke into a kind smile. 'Take a seat, my love. He'll be here in a moment.'

'Thank you.' She perched on the edge of the sofa, unable to take her eyes away from the girl in the picture. The likeness was uncanny. 'Will you be joining me and your husband in the meeting?' she asked, forcing herself to look away from the portrait, and at Mrs Forester.

'My husband?' The woman raised her eyebrows.

'Yes. Will you be joining me and Mr Forester in today's initial discussion?'

Mrs Forester gave a tinkly laugh that Naomi could have sworn she'd heard before. 'Oh no, my dear, he's not my husband.'

'Oh right, sorry.' Naomi cursed herself for making the assumption the pair were married.

'Not a problem. Here he comes.'

She heard footsteps come down the stairs, and prepared to greet her new client as he entered the drawing room.

'Heck!' She stood up, and knocked half her lemonade down her blouse.

'Naomi. It's good to see you. This is the second time we've met, and you've thrown your drink down yourself.'

'You're not Mr Forester!'

Toren laughed, and raked a hand through his silver hair. His brown eyes shone. He looked younger, and healthier, than he had when they'd worked together last year. The weight he'd lost in the run up to the court case had come back on, and he looked athletic, toned, and happy. His light olive skin was tanned and glowing. He was a far cry from the man she had represented last year.

'That I'm not.'

Her mind raced, trying to make sense of what was going on here.

'But you're Mrs Forester.' She widened her eyes at the woman who had shown her in.

'Yes, my dear,' she said with glinting eyes. 'I'm Toren's housekeeper.'

'There isn't a Mr Forester,' Toren

said. 'Jenny here,' he nodded towards Mrs Forester, 'is Pippa's mum, and my temporary housekeeper, while her daughter's globe-trotting. A most fabulous housekeeper she is too, may I add.'

'Pippa still works for you?'

'When Ali went to live with Michelle, she was so upset I thought she needed a break. I suggested she take a year off to do what she'd always longed to do, and go travelling.

'She's working her way round my properties abroad, having a whale of a time. Jenny kindly offered to step in, and help me out in the meantime.'

She stared at him, aware her mouth was wide open, but too shocked to worry about shutting it. 'Toren, what exactly am I doing here?'

'Ah, yes, I have a confession to make.' He walked over to her, took her glass, placed it on the reading table, and held both her hands. 'I might have got you here under false pretences by booking an appointment with you under the name of George Forester.'

'Might have?'

'Okay, I definitely did. But if I'd have given my real name, would you have agreed to see me?'

'That's what you said to me that day in my office,' she murmured.

'Naomi, I stand by what I said to you the night we spent together. I am hopelessly, painfully and desperately in love with you.'

'Toren, it's been nine months.'

He nodded, and rubbed his thumbs over the backs of her fingers. 'I know. A lot has happened in that time. I've moved here for a start.' He tipped his head to show he meant this house. 'I wanted to get everything settled first, before I made contact with you.'

She blinked several times, taking in his words. 'I knew it was Ali in the picture'.

He looked over her head at the portrait. 'Oh yes, of course. That probably gave the game away.'

She turned around to look at the picture, and her eyes filled with tears.

'Does it upset you, looking at her every day when we lost her?'

'You didn't lose me, Naomi.'

The child's voice came from the direction of the archway. She turned her head back towards it, and saw Mrs Forester looking down at the source of the voice.

'Ali!' She broke away from Toren, and rushed over to the little girl. She dropped to her knees, and swooped her up in a bear hug.

'Ow!' Ali laughed. 'Naomi, you're squeezing me to death!'

Naomi released her grip on the girl's waist, and smoothed down her blonde, now longer, curls. 'What are you doing here?'

Toren came over, and rested a hand on Naomi's shoulder. 'Ali's back with me now. Permanently.'

Naomi stood up to face him. 'What? I don't understand. What about her mother? The court case?'

'Michelle did the first decent thing she ever has for her daughter.'

'She let me come and live back with Dad,' Ali clarified.

Naomi looked down at Ali, who had wrapped her arms around her father's waist. 'What? After everything? Why?'

'She could see I wasn't happy, and when I said for the thousandth time I wanted to go back to Dad, she finally let me.'

Naomi turned her attention back to Toren, whose eyes had misted over.

'It's true.' A broad grin stretching across his handsome face.

Ali and Toren's happiness was catching, and she couldn't help but return their smiles.

'Do you know something?' said Mrs Forester, 'Ali's been back for two months now and we've never properly celebrated. Forget the lemonade, I'll get out the champagne. But not for you, I'm afraid, little one.' She gave Ali a fond pat on the head. 'Although I seem to remember I have something special in the freezer for you.' She quickly disappeared back out to the kitchen with Ali skipping close behind her.

'Just us,' said Toren, and took hold of her hands again.

'Just us,' she repeated.

He lowered himself to the ground, resting on one knee.

'Toren!' she gasped, as she realised what he was doing.

He looked up at her. 'Marry me, Naomi. All over again. There's no way I'm letting you go again.'

'For good this time?' She fought to hold her voice steady.

He pressed his lips together, and nodded slowly, never once breaking her gaze. 'For better, for worse.'

She swallowed, and stared back at him. Her throat refused to allow her to form the word she wanted to say. Something was holding her back. Fear of getting hurt all over again?

'No more secrets,' she managed to blurt out just before her voice cracked.

He shook his head, and his eyes shone with tears. 'No more secrets.'

Silence fell.

'Naomi, please,' he laughed shakily, 'Put me out of my misery and give me an answer.'

Funny. She couldn't think of one other occasion when he'd shown nerves.

This really mattered to him.

'Yes!'

'Yes?' He stood up, his eyebrows raised, as if he wasn't sure he'd heard correctly.

'Yes.' She tipped her head up to meet his shining eyes, and reflected his grin with her own.

He wrapped his strong arms around her waist, lifted her off her feet, and spun her around. She screamed out in laughing protest, while he whooped, and ignored her protests entirely.

'What's going on, Dad?' Ali's voice followed the patter of her footsteps, as she headed back into the lounge to see what all the noise was about.

Toren scooped his daughter up in his arms, along with Naomi, and lifted them up together. They both squealed in delight. 'Naomi and I are getting married!'

'Really?' Ali opened her mouth in amazement, and looked from Toren, to Naomi, then back to Toren again. Then she wrapped her arms around both their necks, and sandwiched her head between theirs.

'Does this mean I can call you Mum, Naomi?'

Not wanting to take the liberty of making the decision herself, Naomi looked at Toren.

'I don't see why not,' he said. 'If Naomi's happy with that.'

'I'm very happy with that,' she said, and planted a kiss on Ali's forehead. She thought her heart might burst with happiness.

'Looks like this comes at the perfect time then, my dears.' Jenny appeared with a bottle of champagne, three glasses, and an ice-cream cone. She handed a glass to Toren and Naomi, and gave the ice-cream to Ali. 'Congratulations to you all. What a lovely family you make.'

Warm contentment filled Naomi's body. Yes, we are a family, she thought. An unusual one, perhaps, biologically-speaking.

But what did DNA matter, when they shared something much more important — love.

We do hope that you have enjoyed reading this large print book.

Did you know that all of our titles are available for purchase?

We publish a wide range of high quality large print books including:
Romances, Mysteries, Classics
General Fiction
Non Fiction and Westerns

Special interest titles available in large print are:
The Little Oxford Dictionary
Music Book, Song Book
Hymn Book, Service Book

Also available from us courtesy of Oxford University Press:
Young Readers' Dictionary
(large print edition)
Young Readers' Thesaurus
(large print edition)

For further information or a free brochure, please contact us at:
Ulverscroft Large Print Books Ltd.,
The Green, Bradgate Road, Anstey,
Leicester, LE7 7FU, England.
Tel: (00 44) **0116 236 4325**
Fax: (00 44) **0116 234 0205**

Other titles in the
Linford Romance Library:

LOVE AND LIES

Jenny Worstall

When Rosie Peach arrives for her interview to become Shaston Convent School's new piano teacher, the first person she meets is striking music master David Hart. As her new role gets underway, Rosie comes up against several obstacles: her predecessor Miss Spiker's infamous temper, a bunch of unruly but loveable schoolgirls, and her swiftly growing feelings for David. The nuns of the convent are determined to meddle their way towards a school romance, but David is a complex character, and Rosie can't help but wonder what secrets he is hiding . . .

GAY DEFEAT

Denise Robins

Disarmingly lovely, Delia Beringham is the only daughter of a wealthy financier who indulges her every whim. It is Delia's hope that her lover, Lionel Hewes, will leave his wife for her — but the sudden crash of the Beringham family fortune and her father's suicide change all that. Lionel abruptly fades from the picture, and Delia is left with only her own courage and determination to sustain her. So what is she to say when her father's friend, Martin Revell, chivalrously offers her his hand in marriage?

LORD SAWSBURY SEEKS A BRIDE

Fenella J. Miller

If he is to protect his estate and save his sister from penury, Lord Simon Sawsbury must marry an heiress. Annabel Burgoyne has no desire to marry, but wishes to please her parents, who are offering a magnificent dowry in the hope of enticing an impecunious aristocrat. As Simon and Bella, along with their families, move to their Grosvenor Square residences for the Season, it's not long before the neighbours are drawn together. But when events go from bad to worse, will Simon sacrifice his reputation to marry Bella?

MURDER AT THE HIGHLAND PRACTICE

Jo Bartlett

Shortly after her return to the Scottish Highlands, DI Blair Hannah's small team of detectives is called upon to investigate a suspicious death in the rural town of Balloch Pass. The elderly woman had altered her will before she died, leaving everything to two unlikely beneficiaries: the local priest, and the town's new GP, Dr Noah Bradshaw. As Blair races against time to catch a potential killer, can she beat the ghosts of her past and grab the chance of her own happy ever after?

MACGREGOR'S COVE

June Davies

Running the Bell Inn, which sits high above Macgregor's Cove, is a busy yet peaceful life for Amaryllis's family — but their lodger Kit Chesterton arrives with a heavy secret in tow, which threatens to disturb the quiet waters. Meanwhile, a recent influx in contraband starts ripples of suspicion about smugglers, and Amaryllis's sister sets her sights on Adam Whitlock, who has recently returned from India with a shady companion. Despite the sinister events washing through the Cove, love surfaces as friendship becomes romance and strangers become family.